Bottled Goods

Bottled Goods

a novel

SOPHIE VAN LLEWYN

HARPER ● PERENNIAL

NEW YORK • LONDON • TORONTO • SYDNEY • NEW DELHI • AUCKLAND

HARPER ● PERENNIAL

Originally published in the United Kingdom in 2018 by Fairlight Books.

HarperCollins books may be purchased for educational, business, or sales promotional use. For information, please email the Special Markets Department at SPsales@harper collins.com.

FIRST U.S. EDITION

Library of Congress Cataloging-in-Publication Data has been applied for.

ISBN 978-0-06-297952-0

20 21 22 23 24   LSC   10 9 8 7 6 5 4 3 2 1

*To my father and to the heroes of the
Romanian Revolution of 1989*

Contents

CONTENTS

CONTENTS

The Low People in Our Family

When Aunt Theresa calls, I'm doing my homework on the History of Socialism.

"Alina? Is your mother at home?" she asks.

"No," I say. "She's working the late shift this week. She won't be home until eight."

"Good. I'll pick you up in half an hour. Wear something black and sturdy shoes." And she hangs up before I have the chance to argue.

Half an hour later, the deep horns of her black Volga, similar to a ship's, summon me downstairs. The car has well-defined, voluptuous shapes. The fluffy blanket of snow on its roof makes me think of a curvy woman wearing a rabbit-fur hat. In 1967's Socialist Republic of Romania, this car is the privilege of the Party notables, like my uncle Petru.

Aunt Theresa's hand peeps out of the driver's window. Her wrist is laden with half a dozen gold bracelets that clink merrily when she waves to me. The tips of her fingers clasp a cigarette holder.

My eldest cousin, Matei, is riding shotgun, so

I clamber onto the back seat, where my youngest cousin, Adam, awaits. Between us, on the red upholstery, is a square box with a gliding lid, like the ones that hold the rummy tiles. I wrinkle my nose instantly. The aroma of my aunt's rose perfume doesn't cover the smell of putrefaction.

"Are you wearing black?" asks Aunt Theresa.

I show her the dark wool dress I'm wearing under my thick mantle.

"Good," she says. "Don't open the box."

"Where are we going?" I ask. "And what's that smell?"

"We need to buy some flowers first," she says and drives us to the vegetable market. "Don't tell your mother about this. The low people in our family don't deserve to know."

Matei returns with eight white roses and a small crown, like the ones received by pupils who finish top of the class at the end of the school year. It's made of interwoven bush branches with little round, green leaves. Five plastic carnations are glued on it, like gemstones in a crown.

"Alina, Adam, please open the windows in the back," says Aunt Theresa.

"Where are we going?" I ask again.

"To the Saint George monastery," she says.

My teeth clatter all the way to the monastery, the better part of an hour. Religion is not quite forbidden, but it's something that you don't practice in public, nor speak of. Just like sex.

We've been driving on a bumpy dirt road for a few miles. Adam places one hand on top of the wooden box, steadying it, so it won't fall. I can now see the monastery on top of a hill. Aunt Theresa should park the car—we would then continue by foot. To my surprise, she doesn't stop, but steers left, into the woods. We drive for about ten more minutes on a narrow path, halting in a clearing severed by a frozen creek. I recognize the place. In summer, it's our favorite picnic spot. Behind it, a steep hill where red peonies grow.

Matei fumbles in the trunk and draws out two shovels. He and Adam head for the foot of the hill, and begin to dig. My mouth opens and closes. Aunt Theresa begins to sob noiselessly. Tears are clotting the powder on her cheeks, her mink coat trembles. I hear a rustling of leaves, a creaking of branches and see a priest approaching us. Aunt Theresa walks toward him, kisses his hand. She whispers something to him and he nods.

"Help me," Aunt Theresa says, staring into the open trunk.

I peer over her shoulder. A basket with red wine, a huge ring pretzel baked with honey, *coliva.** I shudder.

"I suspect your mother never told you about your grandfather," she says. "He would have liked

* *Romanian dish made of boiled pearl barley, sugar, and candy, specific to funerals.*

3

an open casket. But we rarely kept him in the bird cage, you see. He liked to walk around the house. He must have fallen. We searched desperately. We found him days after he disappeared, between the living room couch and the wall." A sharp sound, like a banshee shriek, escapes between her sentences. "We found him because of the smell."

The priest and my cousins are standing next to the little hole in the ground, waiting. She gestures for me to grab the basket while she extracts the wooden box from the back seat.

"We came to visit your mother once—and she promised that if we ever come to her house again, she'd tell the authorities where they can find him. The bitch!" She pauses, caressing the lid of the box like the fur of a beloved pet. "You know what—tell her. Tell her I didn't invite her," she says.

*

In the car, Aunt Theresa can't stop speaking. If she stopped, she'd sob, and her eyes would become clouded by tears, and she must watch the road. Night has fallen.

"It was right after the communists came to power," she says. "They were after him—your grandfather had been an important member of the Liberal Party. His friends, they all died while digging the Canal. Killed, beaten, tortured. What was my mother to do? She did what she could, God bless her soul.

She shrunk him. *Your* mother—she wanted to have nothing to do with him. Nothing." Her voice rises in the cigarette smoke that's clouding the interior of the Volga. "She never came to see him—not even once. And the fool, how he missed her!"

The smell of putrefaction lingers in the over-heated car. I mean to ask her how my grandmother shrunk him, but I don't want to interrupt.

Glazed Apples

The beach is sun in Alina's eyes, sand in her hair, salt tightening her skin like a dress she has outgrown, smell of spoiled salted fish. The beach is a conglomerate of eyes glazing her as if she were an apple, making her feel constrained and sticky with their lust. The view from her room is a cement wall barely three feet from her window, but what did she expect when she is allowed to stay for free in a three-star hotel for an entire month, in one of Romania's most luxurious resorts?

Until this summer of 1969, the sea was a mystery, the "seaside"—a dreaded word. It spoke of her mother's lament: *I wish we had enough money to take you with us*, uttered with a poorly hidden smile from the corner of her mouth. It spoke of a long drive to her grandmother's, where she was forgotten until the leaves turned brown and school started. It spoke of dusty side streets, screaming children and their cruel games, knees covered in dried blood, bathing every other day in a plastic tub where her legs barely fit.

This summer, Alina is a translator and a tour guide for the German tourists at her hotel. She is relieved whenever they decide to leave the beach and see some sights. The tourists, too loud, too cheerful, too inquisitive at the resort, become her adoring audience.

To the right, she tells them with a smile as if she's giving away state secrets, *is the Museum of History and Archaeology, the former City Hall.* The Germans gape at her and ask pointed questions, to show they have been listening. They are schoolchildren again, and she is their mistress. In the narrow corridor of the bus, she tells them about the wonders of communism.

She says, *We will be visiting a special shop for tourists now. You can find Western products there, if you miss them. I am not allowed to come in with you.*

They ask, *How is it to live in a land without freedom? To stay outside and stare at the windows?*

She says with a crooked smile, *Nobody lacks anything in this country. Do your youngsters receive an apartment as soon as they are married? Is unemployment a problem in your country? Does your Leader have your best interests at heart?*

They say, *Leader or not, how about Mars and Toblerone chocolates? Wolford stockings, Italian shoes?*

Alina laughs. *I would readily give up my chocolate if that helps eradicate poverty.*

They don't believe her. They rain chocolates and cigarettes on her when they return. She keeps the chocolates to herself and the cigarettes she gives to

Liviu, the other German-speaking tour guide. In her newly gained confidence among the Germans' rosy cheeks, beer bellies, and pale-blond hair, she feels like an older sister to this lanky boy with a wispy, thin moustache. He never stares at her bosom or at her legs, like the others do. He always looks her in the eyes when he is talking to her, in a hardly audible, serious tone.

My mother died when I was a child, he says. *I want to become an archaeologist. I hate being with so many people all day, but I need the money. When I get to my hotel room, my head is pounding. I would like to sell the cigarettes you give me, but I enjoy them too much.*

But the tourists have come for the beach, so Alina plays the fearless tour guide no more than two full days per week and sometimes a few hours in the morning. The rest of the time, she must do like all the others and brew on the hot sand, like a Turkish coffee.

Liviu comes to the beach one day, and she chats with him and even takes a few puffs from his cigarette. He shields her from the unpleasant stares, and she wants him to come more often. In the evening, his skin is crayfish red and he has to brush cold yogurt on it for days, making the sensible German noses in the bus curl up at the smell of sour milk.

On her last day as a tour guide, they are walking on the promenade at Constanța, the Germans in front, she and Liviu lagging behind like two jaded shepherds.

Alina is bored of saying, *This is the statue of our greatest national poet. This was once a splendid casino.* Instead, she leans against the lacy railings and peers at the sea breaking in millions of pearls of foam beneath her. The sea, only the sea, with its push and pull, its restlessness, its rustling sounds, she loves. Liviu lays his hand on top of hers.

He says, *I kept all the packs from the cigarettes you gave me and made a coffee table. I have no idea how I will carry it back home.*

Dear Father Frost

I know that I am twenty and almost a married woman, but I'm very willing to believe in you again, if you would consider bringing me one single item from the list below. In return, I promise you eternal love and devotion. I would preach in your name on the streets, even though it's forbidden and I might be picked up by the Police or the Secret Services to be beaten and administered electric shocks to banish all popular and religious beliefs from my head. I would use your real name, the one you had before 1948, when the Communist Party came to power: Father C. Just bring me one single item and I'm sure that we can reach an agreement regarding payment. Please. Even half an item. Anything.

Wishlist:

- A pair of Levi's blue jeans.

- A red lipstick, like the one the piano teacher is wearing, that elegant shade of burgundy.

- Better yet than the two items above, a pair of new boots. The soles of my black boots are so worn, that they're very slippery when it rains—I fell two times last week. I don't want to think what will happen when it snows.

- Even better, a portable electric stove I can use in my room. I'm sick of cooking all of my food by using the immersion heater.

- A raise, so I can buy all of the above and send a little something extra to Liviu. Why do teachers' salaries have to be so low?

- My fiancé. Help him finish college this year, not the next. This month. Today.

- Please make my mother change her mind and support me through college so I can become a translator, instead of having to confront eight-year-olds every single day for the rest of my life.

- Please turn back time to that moment when I introduced her to Liviu. Please don't let her throw me out of the house.

- Please make me a child again. A teenager. A student. A girl who hasn't lost her father yet or her romantic views concerning the world, poverty, kindness, a parent's love.

Please unmake me a grown-up.
Please don't let me down.

All the love in the world,
Alina

Prima Noctis

This woman in the stained wedding dress is not really Alina, bending over Liviu as he searches for blankets in a huge wooden trunk at the foot of his parents' bed. Her ankle-long tulle veil should not have been covered with dust, after being trampled under so many rubber-soled boots, hardened bare feet. Her head should not have been spinning from all the whirling on the dance floor, or from the homemade plum schnapps, or from struggling to understand what was being said to her in the strange mountain dialect. It was not a wedding, but a documentary about customs and traditions that she had been watching, trapped inside the bride's body. Not only had the guests at the ceremony been so queer and unfamiliar, even her Liviu looked foreign in the traditional costume he changed into shortly before midnight.

"Are you even listening?" asks her husband.

"Huh?"

"The carpets hanging on the walls. My grandmother made them," he says. "She had an Austrian weaving loom. It was a huge, beautiful thing. When the communists came to power, they took her weaving loom, her lands, and her husband."

"Liviu, I don't need a history lesson right now," says Alina. "Keep it for your class."

She doesn't want to remember that their family histories grew in parallel realities. When the communists came, two years before Alina was born, her mother and her aunt Theresa lived in a mansion in Bucharest, complete with a team of eight servants and their former governess. Alina is glad that her mother refused to accept the convergence of histories and come to the wedding. It was enough that Aunt Theresa had come, the golden bracelets at her wrist jingling to the rhythm of the traditional wedding songs as Liviu's brother spun her on the dance floor. Her aunt, in spite of her benign, well-humored look, made Alina feel ashamed of the heavy, bug-eaten furniture in her father-in-law's house, of its floors made of compacted earth, of the dust covering the streets like an ill-willed layer of snow, of the men's queer accents and their bawdy jokes, of their fingers stained with grease from the liquid oozed by the cabbage rolls, of their onion-and-cheap-alcohol breaths that came too close, too close to her face as they danced with her, kissed her on the cheeks, hugged her.

Liviu is done raising his eyebrows and takes another blanket out of the trunk, tossing it on the bed, on top of the others.

"Don't we have enough? You already pulled out three."

"It can get really cold at night," he says. "Besides, I was looking for some clean sheets."

The soft inflections of his dialect forgotten, Liviu talks again like the history student he was when they met. Back then, his eyes became glassy and began dancing in their sockets when he told her about Dacian excavation sites discovered in the heart of Transylvania.

Alina sweeps her hand over the rugs on the walls. They're rectangular, with a geometrical pattern in red, white, and black, a form of controlled chaos. A thick layer of dust, like talc, has seeped through the fabric, and it now glues to the skin of her palm, where so many layers of sweat have dried. Her dress is just as sticky as the rest of her, and makes her think of Hercules's poisoned shirt.

"Can you please help me get out of this dress?" she asks, turning, but he is no longer in the room. "Liviu?"

"In here," he calls from the main chamber.

Alina follows him and sees the blankets and sheets tossed on the narrow, plain bed across from the hearth. She points toward the pile.

"What's this?"

"We're sleeping in here," he says.

"Why?"

"I can't spend my wedding night in my parents' bed," he says, recoiling and pursing his lips. "It's disgusting."

Alina is too tired to argue. She turns, pointing at the hidden zipper that runs across her back. As Liviu's greasy fingers, clumsied by wine, stray along her spine, she closes her eyes. He could be any of the men who had been at the wedding feast, with their blackened feet, coarse beards, rough hands, but now she is as dirty as any of them, a princess dragged through the mud. The day lingers on her skin, in the sweat mixed with dust and frankincense smoke, cabbage and garlic vapors from the kitchen, and she is not Alina. Maybe she is one of her noble ancestors, a spoiled girl held hostage by a peasant, and his callused hands are tearing the dress off her, throwing her on his humble bed, and there she lies, trembling, eyes half closed, waiting for the prick.

A Flower and Two Gardeners

Dear Diary,

Today we saw the last of my brother-in-law
for at least three weeks. Honestly, I'm relieved
that Liviu and I will finally be alone. It's not
that I don't like him, but when Mihai started
visiting every evening, it became too much. I
haven't cuddled with Liviu on the sofa in nearly
two months, just the two of us, browsing the
Bulgarian and Serbian stations. Our evenings
at home are pretty much the same: Liviu and
Mihai go into the kitchen after dinner so Mihai
can smoke, while I sit on one of the living room
armchairs with a book in my hands, too tired
to read, aching for conversation. Sometimes,
they can be bothered to wash their own plates,
but mostly, they leave them on the dining room
table for me to clean up after Mihai heads
home. I hate that—dipping my hands in the
cold water when I should have been wrapped
in a blanket, sprawled in my own bed.

They spend their evenings at the kitchen table, popping sunflower seeds, while Mihai is smoking. I can hear Liviu coughing, and I tell him it's his brother's fault, but he denies it. Once, I picked up one of Mihai's cigarettes and lit it, and Liviu was really angry. He told me to put it down, that it's not ladylike, not like me. *It doesn't become you.* I was angry too, because, for a moment, he sounded just like my mother, and I'm tired of being told what I should and shouldn't do, of dreading the punishment.

Mihai invited us to the movies tonight and introduced us to his newest girlfriend. He booked seats at *A Flower and Two Gardeners*. That's a really romantic and sappy Bollywood movie, so I was surprised that he took us too. I mean, when Somna's husband saves the life of the child she had with her lover, that's the perfect moment to huddle into your date, seeking comfort. As it was, my sharp gray eye was constantly glaring at this new girl whose name I forgot, at Mihai's hand finding his way up that long, beautiful mantle of hers, toward her thighs and the purple-colored skirt barely covering them. Oh, the mantle. She took a plain black cloth and painted an abstract pattern on it, but it looked very artsy, very chic. She's an art student, she said. She also said that she'd paint one of my mantles too, but I think that was the last we'll see of

her. I doubt she knows that Mihai is leaving
for his vacation in France tomorrow.

After the movie, he dropped her off at her
house and came by our place. He sat on the
floor on a huge pillow and told us how he met
her at the market, how her parents are farmers
and unrelenting churchgoers—the kind that
go to church in spite of the fact that the Secret
Services pick them up for questioning every
other week after Sunday service. What he said
made me wonder how deceiving appearances
can be and what Liviu and his brother usually
talk about, behind the closed kitchen door. I
like to think it's universal truths deemed too
dirty for my ears. Liviu protects me too much
from the outside world. I'm afraid that one
of these days the dam he built will break
and all the world's ugliness will spill out
and drown me.

When I started to yawn, thinking about
my classes tomorrow, Mihai went downstairs
and brought a plastic bag from his car. In it
were (extravagant) gifts for us: a Nina Ricci
perfume for me and a pair of Levi's jeans for
Liviu. After Mihai left, Liviu told me that
his brother had sold his apartment last week
so he can go to France. I told my husband
how stupid I thought this was—Liviu just
shrugged and said, *It's Mihai. He'd give
anything and anyone up for his dreams.*

I told him I would never do anything like that. Liviu clicked his tongue and said I know nothing about being poor and desperate. That's when I caught fire. I told him that although I didn't have a crappy childhood like he did, I had to work my ass off to help him finish college after my mother kicked me out and live in a boarding school room for two years. I told him that, anyway, it's beside the point, selling the apartment wasn't a last resort, just his brother's whim. Liviu said, *I'm sorry you had to do all that. Trust me, I'm grateful to you, but I'm also a bit sick of you bringing that up all the time.*

That's when I slammed the door and told him to screw himself.

I can't sleep now. Liviu upset me too much. And I keep thinking about those jeans Liviu got from his brother. The Levi's jeans were *my* dream. If I didn't have to help my husband through college, I could have saved up for a pair of jeans.

I deserve them. I earned them. Tomorrow I'll wake up before Liviu does and try them on. If I am lucky, they will fit.

The Saturday When
Everything Changed

6:30 a.m.

Alina wakes up, brushes her teeth, applies unobtrusive makeup for school (a dust of powder and lipstick in a soft brown tone). On her way to the kitchen, where she will make the coffee, she wakes Liviu up with a soft caress on his arm.

Nothing has changed.

7:25 a.m.

Alina, wearing a dark-blue pencil skirt and a white shirt with short sleeves, makes her way to school. Before the doors to the school are thrown open for the pupils, she has time to drink another cup of coffee with her fellow teachers in their break room. Miss Puiu, the music teacher, always comes in at 7:30 and makes coffee for all the staff. The coffee is as diluted and discolored as herself: her clothes, her hair, even the memories of her sad childhood, which now don't impress her audience anymore from too much telling. This morning, Miss Puiu repeats the story about how she and her seven siblings were only allowed to have milk with their polenta on Sundays. Everybody kindles their own thoughts, humming and nodding as they pretend to listen.

Before class begins, Alina and the children sing "The Tricolor Flag," the national anthem, while looking admiringly at the picture of Ceauşescu. From above the blackboard, the Beloved Leader smiles, watching over them like a big brother.

Nothing has changed.

10:45 a.m.

Alina assigns the homework in Romanian for Monday. This time the children have to write an essay explaining why books are their friends. She wishes them a nice day.

Nothing has changed.

11:20 a.m.

Though Liviu will not come for hours, Alina already prepares herself. She puts on a lime-yellow dress that ends a palm's width above her knee. She uses a dark-blue pencil for her mismatched eyes (it works with both gray and hazel) and the burgundy-red Helena Rubinstein lipstick, the one Liviu gave her for her birthday. She dabs a little on her cheeks.

When she is done, she sinks onto the armchair in the living room, a historical novel in her hands, *The Soimaresti Family*. She glances every few minutes at the door. She reads page 127 eight times. She should be working on the math problems she has to prepare for the textbook.

Nothing has changed.

2:10 p.m.

Alina calls her mother. They discuss the neighbor's daughter, Alexandra. She is a childhood friend of Alina's who has just run off with a married man. "Run off" is one way of describing what happened ("eloped," to borrow a term from Alina's mother, is another), but the truth is far less romantic than what might seem to be a page from a Victorian novel. The two live in Alexandra's one-bedroom flat, a few blocks away from the married man's former home. After sufficient *ooh's* and *aah's*, "Her poor mother" and "Who would have thought?" have been spoken, Alina's mother invites her daughter to have lunch with her. Alina refuses, saying she has plans. Alina's mother is offended and tells her daughter that she only comes by when she needs something. This is unfair, but before Alina has the chance to say so, her mother has already hung up. Fortunately, Alina has no time to be wistful, because Liviu finally arrives.

Alina grabs her white vinyl purse. Liviu wraps his arm around her shoulder, and she caresses his hand with the tips of her nails, manicured in an oval shape.

At the restaurant, Liviu orders schnitzel with chips. He cuts the schnitzel in bite-size chunks and the chips in halves. By the time he starts eating, Alina has devoured half of her *kievskaia** and is taking small bites, combining the chicken, the pickled cucumbers, and bell peppers on the tip of the fork. She begins making small talk, even though she knows that will slow Liviu even more.

"Rodica wrote to me this week."

Liviu hums.

"You know, Rodica, who coordinates the textbook we are working on. She says that my math problems are very clever, and that I need to start publishing a few. In math journals for elementary and middle school."

Liviu grunts while chewing very slowly on the tender meat.

"Do your teeth hurt again?"

"Uh-uh."

"I never thought about that. Getting published, I mean. Rodica says I have to make a bit of a name for myself. Before the textbook comes out."

"Yes, honey. Do that."

"When is your brother coming back from France? We haven't seen him in a while. In more than a month."

Liviu wipes a bit of grease from the corner of his mouth with the linen napkin. "The chief inspector told me yesterday that he sent all the papers to Bucharest, to the Ministry for Education. They should be confirming me as an adjunct headmaster in a few weeks."

Alina claps her hands. "Eeee! That's great! I'm so glad!"

---

* Stuffed chicken breast, filled with pickled vegetables, coated with eggs and bread crumbs, then fried.

"I'm taking you out for another treat today. How about a marquise cake at Tosca?"

Alina's smile freezes a little. She was thinking about a different kind of treat. Those Levi's jeans, eluding her since high school.

Nothing has changed.

4:40 p.m.

As they approach their home, Alina falls silent. The thought that she has not worked on her math problems, not even a single one, is nagging her. Liviu will want to make love, and she cannot put him off.

In front of their blockhouse, two men in gray suits in spite of all the summer around them are waiting. Alina is wary. When the men take a few steps to meet them, Alina can feel her heart thumping in her ears.

One of the men, the short, balding one, grabs Liviu by the flesh underneath his elbow, burying his fingers into it, and says, "Please come with us. We have to ask you a few questions."

Liviu tries to yank his arm free, but the thick fingers that look like drumsticks dig even deeper.

"What is this about?"

"Please. Don't make a scene. Come with us."

"Please," says Alina, putting her moist hand above the bald man's. "Please. He has done nothing wrong. He couldn't have." Her world is a blur as she begins to lose control over her tears.

The taller of the two men in suits takes her gently aside and says, "No, he hasn't, comrade. He just has to answer some questions. We have reason to believe that your husband's brother will never return from France."

Everything has changed.

Alina's Mother

Alina's mother likes to put her fur hat on half an hour before she has to leave for work. Fur looks as natural on her as if she has grown it herself. The fur is white with gray tips, and Alina doesn't remember which animal it once belonged to.

Alina's mother swirls the green telephone cord around her finger while she talks to the headmaster, calling in sick for her daughter. To some women, these things come naturally.

Alina's mother says, *Stay put. Don't leave the house. When I come back from work, I'll bring your favorite records. Make me a list.*

Alina's mother doesn't call the entire day. Alina cowers under a blanket in her mother's house, wondering if she will ever see Liviu again, wishing she were no older than eight.

Alina's mother brings her the records: Phoenix and the Beatles and ABBA. They are playing in the background while Alina and her mother cook beef medallions in red sauce. Alina is preparing the mashed potatoes. Alina's mother swings her hips to the rhythm of "Waterloo" and Alina means to tell her that it is bad taste to be so cheerful while she is hurting, but even at twenty-six, she's still a bit in awe of her.

Alina's mother places the plate with the medallions on the table without spilling a single drop. Alina scoops a piece of meat, bleeding sauce on the yellow tablecloth. Her mother frowns. *Really, Alina, at your age.*

Alina says, *Stop exaggerating! In this house, everything is a catastrophe,* more shrilly than intended.

The thin, rounded eyebrows of Alina's mother shoot upward. *Look, dear, I know you worry about Liviu, but you shouldn't make a scene out of everything. Is that what you learned in our house?*

Alina stabs at her piece of meat furiously. Alina's mother says, *When and if he ever comes out alive, take care. Don't do anything foolish. I'll be watching.*

Crumbs

Alina waits for ten minutes before knocking again on the metal door. Today, she's late. She had to feel her way with the tip of her boot in the darkness. The slush from yesterday turned into ice and, to save power, the city lights went off at three o'clock in the morning. Every Sunday, at six o'clock sharp, she has to be at the back door of the bakery, waiting for Mrs. Popescu to hand her a plastic bag. The bag contains steaming bread, cheese pies, and sometimes apple strudels. Liviu loves apple strudels.

Liviu often tells her about the apple strudels his mother baked for them every Sunday. It is one of his dearest memories. After she died, he was the one who had to cook for his younger siblings.

"At fourteen, I could have written a cookbook by myself," he says with a smile he doesn't mean.

*

The door creaks, and a shy streak of light scares the darkness away. The bonneted head of Mrs. Popescu appears and a chubby hand offers the bag. Alina begins searching for her wallet, but the baker is already closing the door. Alina only has time to slip in a quick "thank you." Mrs. Popescu never takes her money, but Mrs. Popescu's daughter, Carmen, is in Alina's class. Alina overlooks minor mistakes in Carmen's homework and tests. Last year, Alina would never have done anything like this. But she needs the apple strudels.

Since the chief inspector summoned him to his office, apple strudels are one of the few things that still make Liviu smile.

"Comrade Mungiu, my sincere congratulations. We hear nothing but the best about your methods. You are one of the most capable history teachers in the county," the chief inspector said.

Liviu replied with a gleeful "thank you" to the first kind words he'd heard in weeks. Since his brother had fled the country, his friends were avoiding him and the authorities were harassing him.

"Your motherland needs you at Seceratu, comrade Mungiu," the inspector continued. "I sincerely hope that you will not fail her."

The peasants in Seceratu were notorious in the county for having the highest dropout rates in elementary school. They had no use for a history teacher.

Not even her aunt Theresa, with her high connections, could rescue Liviu from Seceratu.

"My hands are tied," she had said, the gold bracelets on her thin wrist chiming merrily. "They'd been clever. Disguised it as an honor. It would be an offense not to accept this position. Or would you rather be working in the fields?"

*

Alina's breaths are fog clouds melting in the darkness. If she could distinguish colors, she would see that her fingertips are purple. She left her gloves at home and can't keep her hands in her pockets because she has to use them for balance. She walks by the CEC Bank, by the town plaza, by countless gray buildings. At the vegetable market, she notices a dozen people standing in line in front of a butcher's shop.

"Are they getting a delivery today?" Alina asks a toothless man.

"Minced lamb and beef, they said. That lady with the fur hat in front of the line, she knows one of the men who work behind the counter."

"Lamb and beef!"

She could make stuffed eggplant with the lamb and the beef. Moussaka. Meat pies. The possibilities are overwhelming, so Alina stops and stands in line. The line is like a train with many, many wagons.

Liviu rides the train, too. Three hours every day. When he comes home, Liviu smells of alcohol.

"Everybody on the train drinks," he says. "If I don't drink, they call me snobbish."

*

Dawn is cracking. Alina swaps the plastic bag between her hands, placing the free hand into her pocket. Dozens of people have gathered behind her. The line looks like a fidgety snake. The passersby stop and place themselves at the back of the line, waiting patiently for the doors to open.

Alina always opens the door when Liviu comes home. She keeps looking out the window, watching for him. He doesn't kiss her anymore when he arrives, but she doesn't mind. The smell of alcohol makes her nauseated. She also dislikes the silence settling between them like frost, so during dinner, Alina makes winding monologues.

*

When she finally arrives at the front of the line, the butcher is already out of pork, but there is still minced lamb. There never was any beef.

At home, Liviu wrinkles his nose when he sees the strudel.

"It's stiff and cold," he says.

"I bought lamb," she says and remembers she wanted to buy eggplants.

Alina takes her gloves and heads back out into the cold.

When she returns from the vegetable market, all that is left in the plastic bag are crumbs and a few oily napkins.

Strigoi

Outside, the air is blow-dryer hot. As soon as she arrives at Aunt Theresa's, Alina asks for water.

"Or even better, your special drink, the one you make with jasmine, black tea, and your secret ingredient."

Aunt Theresa points at the glass cabinet in her living room. At first, Alina thinks she's pointing at the cat, Absala, standing on it like an Egyptian statue of itself: fine-wristed and sleek, even though its color, white with dark patches like stains, gives it away as a former stray. Alina moves to pet it.

"I can't," says Theresa. "I can't touch the glassware, not unless I want to let the *strigoi** back in."

Alina notices that all the cups and glasses are turned upside down. She chuckles. "You almost had me. Water would be fine."

But Aunt Theresa isn't smiling. She fumbles in one of the cupboard's drawers, extracts a basil branch and a bottle filled with transparent liquid

* *Troubled spirit of the dead, rising from the grave (Romanian folklore).*

that seems to catch the sunlight and make it glow golden. Alina stands up. Her hand hovers above one of the crystal glasses.

"Don't!" shouts Aunt Theresa. "We barely kicked it out of our house two days ago. None of us could sleep last week—can't you see?" Aunt Theresa points at her own eyes. But the signs of fatigue have been well hidden under powder and concealer—or she may have slept her exhaustion off. She places the bottle and the branch on the low coffee table, then delves in her purse. "Serves me right for trying to help a friend."

Aunt Theresa pours the liquid onto a saucer, dips her keys into it.

"A *strigoi*?" asks Alina, with an improvised smile. She tries to laugh at her aunt, but she knows that Theresa's playing with the supernatural is often a dance on the brink of a precipice, and nobody has any idea what awaits below.

"Yes. A friend's—former friend's—great-uncle. What they did to the poor man! I'd come back to haunt them, too, if I were him! But, of course, he can't find them now. Not anymore. So he haunts us. Though it's not much: slamming windows and doors, scattering our clothes or the garbage, breaking dishes, just enough to be an annoyance. But if he finds my friend—ha! The things he can do!" Aunt Theresa sucks in her cheeks. She looks like a rosy-cheeked Mommy.

"I thought vampires sucked blood, not the *strigoi*," says Alina.

"No, the *strigoi* drain life. Anyhow, it was ill-considered to summon him at my house. No matter, Father Toma is coming down from Putna tomorrow, and will help me fix this. Be a good girl and stretch your hands now."

Aunt Theresa dips her hands into the saucer and rubs Alina's wrists, making the sign of the cross. "Holy water. Told you not to come here today; you insisted. It's such a bother to get out—and I really need to. We need more of this, we're running out."

When Alina called her, Aunt Theresa did warn her against coming—but with the heat outside, and Liviu coming late in the evening from Seceratu, Alina couldn't bear staying in her flat a moment longer, stifling in the heat and her own fears. Even a *strigoi* was safe, compared to what could have happened in her own home.

"We're going for a drive," says Aunt Theresa. "But first, we have to get out of the house. When I say 'now' you have to move very fast. Very, very, fast, all right?"

Alina shrugs. This is not the strangest thing she's witnessed in her aunt's house. Theresa wets the tips of her basil branch and uses it to spray holy water on the door, on the frame, on the threshold. Absala follows them, swooshing her tail. Alina points at the cat.

"Don't worry, she just wants to guard the door," says Aunt Theresa, then places the holy-water bottle in her purse. She squeezes the doorknob. "Now!"

Alina and her aunt tumble outside. Alina's left foot catches in the doormat, and she lands on her knees. Aunt Theresa slams the door shut behind them, then helps Alina up. "The *strigoi*, that's why you fell. And that's the least of what he can do." Theresa shudders. "Poor man."

Much later, her aunt's elegant Volga trembles with all its joints on a road full of potholes. The avenue of trees framing the road casts long, thin shadows, and between them the asphalt glints silver, shivering. Alina thinks of oases in the desert, of light and its reflection. She finally asks, "And the glasses? Why were they turned upside down?"

"The *strigoi* tries to use any concave object to get into the house and wreak havoc. We've been eating and drinking off flat plates for days."

Aunt Theresa veers onto an earthen path. Yellow dust powders the car's windows. Alina thinks how nice it would be to emerge on the other side of the dirt storm, into a different reality, one where the authorities aren't persecuting Liviu for his brother's defection, where she doesn't have to tremble every time she comes home for fear that two agents of the Secret Services are waiting for her, where she and Liviu are as light and carefree as they were last year. She thinks how her life has been turned upside down, too, like Aunt Theresa's glasses, and how there is no Father Toma she could ask to exorcise the evil spirits that have a grip on her life.

How to Attract (Unwanted) Attention from the Communist Authorities

1. Linger in the classroom, leafing through the class roster—though you could do this just as well (even better, with the lack of interjections and other noises of eight-year-olds) in the teacher's break room.

2. Insist on lingering, even when noticing the first signs of trouble.

Signs of trouble:

a. Pupil Săpunaru Carmen, the most popular girl in class—who just presented her new pencil box, fully equipped with secret drawers, compartments, a lid from which a princess with a lime-green dress and blue hair smiles mockingly—is gathering her belongings.

b. The crowd of adorers is clearing from around her, migrating toward open spaces (for instance, the hallways or the school-yard), where they can more effectively burn the excess energy they always seem to display.

c. Pupil Atanasiu Maria, wearing a uniform inherited from one of her three older siblings, is watching pupil Săpunaru with the fixed stare of a deer who is about to be run over by a truck.

d. The former finally decides to leave the safety of her desk and engage the latter in conversation.

e. The diva seems to be giving monosyllabic answers as the other speaks in low tones, with a bowed head. The admirer is becoming increasingly nervous (this state to be recognized by the compulsive scratching of the scalp).

f. The follower pushes something colorful, that appears to be some kind of magazine, under the nose of the revered one.

3. Raise your eyes from the class roster and watch the scene unfolding before you, dumb-struck. Don't move or say anything as the diva pushes her admirer back, the colorful

object falling to the ground. Or as the crazed fan gathers the crumpled item from the floor, almost as wounded as her pride. By now you have identified the apple of discord as a *Pif et Hercule* magazine, a contraband article forbidden by the government.

4. When it is far too late to pretend nothing has happened, close the class roster and take hurried steps toward the door. Stop on the threshold, when you can no longer ignore the prima donna's cries of "Comrade teacher!"

5. Say, "Yes, what is it?" in a tone as snappy as you can, hoping (vainly and groundlessly) to intimidate.

6. At the diva's excited exclamations of "Atanasiu brought a forbidden magazine to class!," simply raise an eyebrow.

7. Now say, "I don't see anything," without looking at the zealot's blue apron. Through its thin and discolored fabric, the sharp corners of the magazine are peeking and the familiar contours of the two silly pets can be made out.

8. Ignore the entreaties and exclamations of, "It's there, under her clothes! How come you don't see it?"

9. Step a bit back and to the side, so that the perpetrator may escape through the open door and make her way (hopefully) toward a garbage bin. Preferably one that is not located on the school grounds. Don't call for the perpetrator as she runs away.

10. In fact, don't do anything, except walk toward the teacher's break room, heart banging in your chest like an angry neighbor when you've been playing loud music for hours, the huge class roster tucked under your arm, the sneak's cries in the line of "I'll tell my daddy about this! You saw it. I know you did" ringing in your ears. Her father is high in the Police. You're heading toward a head-on collision with the Secret Services and their like. Congratulations!

Quotes from My Mother (Commented)—Part I

"You would never even have thought of doing something like this! It's all Liviu's fault. I told you not to marry that man! Him and his family of reactionaries!"

This statement was my mother's first response when I told her about the incident with the magazine.

Her assertion was wrong on so many levels:

- Liviu was definitely *not* in the classroom when I decided to turn a blind eye to what was happening.

- Liviu's family was far poorer and less politically involved than ours. None of his close relatives happened to be a prominent member of the Liberal Party or of the Conservative Party or of any party whatsoever (unlike my grandfather). His grandfather's only fault had been trying to resist the collectivization (the posh term for "the communist government took the peasants' lands away from them"). For this reason, he was awarded a two-year stay in a dungeon.

- Liviu doesn't even know about what I've done. I mean to tell him, and I will, one of these days. I just couldn't find it in myself to burden him with this, too. I don't want him to think that what I did will cause even more trouble for him. I'm sure that's what he'll say. Lately, he only thinks of himself.

I didn't make any of the points above while discussing the matter with my mother, because:

a. It would have been pointless. Everything I do wrong is Liviu's fault anyway.
b. I had more pressing matters to debate, like what to do next.
c. I was so panicked and relieved at the same time after I had admitted to what I had done that I didn't think about any of the counter arguments above, except for the last one.

"And the magazine fell on the floor?" Whistles. "And you're still not sure what it was? Was it a *Pif et Hercule* or not? How can I help you if you don't tell me the truth?"

Yes, the magazine fell. Yes, I pretended not to see it, not even when pupil Atanasiu concealed it clumsily under her clothing. Yes, it was definitely a *Pif et Hercule*, but I suddenly remembered that my apartment might be tapped. I do stupid things when I panic.

Regarding the last question: point taken. I turned the water tap on in the kitchen and whispered the truth in my mother's ear.

"This is bad. This is the worst thing you've ever done."

This particular observation made my already racing pulse skyrocket and my self-possession dissolve into tears—I had been holding them back for the entire duration of our conversation.

"Maybe your aunt Theresa could help you. At least, she could tell you if you're in trouble or not."

I was actually thinking about the same thing, but I loathe asking people for favors, even more when they're family. But now that my mother has mentioned Aunt Theresa (and they haven't spoken in years), it seems like the only option I have.

"You wouldn't have gotten into this kind of trouble if it weren't for your husband, though."

I'm starting to believe this.

"You have to show *them* where you stand. If you do the right thing, I'm sure they'll leave you alone."

Yes, but what to do? Isn't it a bit late now to report pupil Atanasiu, more than a week after the incident? What if my mother's wrong and the Secret Services aren't going to do anything about it? It's been a week, and nothing has happened. Except for the fact that the pupil in question hasn't come to school since the incident.

"When is your math book coming out?"

Deciding there was nothing left to say about my slip with the magazine, my mother changed the subject and, hard to believe as it may seem, she managed to make me even more nervous than I already was. Rodica from Bucharest, the project coordinator for the math exercise book, hasn't returned my calls in weeks.

"Has your mother been in here again?" Fake coughing. (He likes to parade his cigarette intolerance, which was nonexistent when his brother smoked, and disapproval of everything my mother does.) Waving of hand, cutting through imaginary smoke. "I don't want her in my house."

This was a quote by Liviu when he came home. I had to prepare the meat for the *rasol** we were having for dinner. I was in a hurry after my mother left, so I forgot to gather the remnants of our coffee and

* *Romanian dish made of beef, boiled in salted water, along with vegetables and potatoes.*

cake from the coffee table. Liviu found the incriminating evidence.

Regarding the question: Yes. My mother has visited me.

Regarding the statement: Liviu, there are so many things I don't like about you, too.

Homework

"Atanasiu Maria, to the blackboard!" says Alina, staring at the child's worn and thin apron that failed to conceal contraband merchandise last week.

"Yes, comrade teacher."

"Please underline the subjects and the predicates." Alina points toward the sentences glowing in white chalk.

"Yes, comrade teacher."

Maria turns her reddened eyes away and looks imploringly at the Beloved Leader's picture that hangs above the blackboard. Twenty years later, an icon of the Savior will hang in this spot, but in 1975, it's Ceaușescu's depiction that the children must revere.

The pupil begins scratching underlines with a scrape of chalk as big as a fingernail. Her sleeve slips as she reaches on the tip of her toes for the first sentence. Alina can see that Maria's forearm is full of blue-and-purple blotches on her fair skin. She turns away and opens the window.

"It's stifling in here," she murmurs.

She crosses her arms and looks at the old lady selling flowers on the corner of the street. The woman ties her head-kerchief. On it, beige snails are printed on a brown background. The snails, with their continuous revolving motion around their own axis, make Alina feel dizzy. She cannot bear to look. She closes the window and turns to see that Maria has finished the exercise.

"Hmm," she grunts. "Good. Now please write down the main ideas from the text you had to prepare for today, 'Ştefan the Great and the Peasants of the Tall Oak.'"

Maria looks down at the painted planks of the dais, her hands collected in front of her. Alina's eyebrows shoot upward.

"Pupil Atanasiu? The text?"

"I'm sorry, comrade Mungiu, but I did not prepare anything."

"Why?"

"I did not know we had to prepare the text, comrade Mungiu."

"Oh? You did not come to school for nearly a week, and you couldn't be bothered to ask about your homework, either?"

Alina is very much aware of the fact that Maria has no friends in class she could ask anything.

"I'm sorry, comrade Mungiu."

The girl's voice is wobbly, like an unstable object, ready to fall at the slightest gust of wind.

Alina turns her eyes toward the class roster and

the pupil's grade report. She paints the mark in two swift moves. The four looks like a desolate upturned chair next to the straight tens in Maria's column.

"Atanasiu, get back to your place."

Alina can hear the girl weeping when she sees the grade, but she covers her sobs with her own voice.

"Open your textbooks to page forty-three. Today we will talk about the past tense."

*

During the break, Alina seeks a quiet spot behind the gym. A few of the older students are smoking there and scurry away as soon as they see her. She leans against the cold wall and wishes she had asked them for a cigarette. When she closes her eyes, the blue-and-purple spots on Maria's forearm twirl before her eyes, a madman's juggling balls.

*

Alina spends the last break of the day in the teachers' room. She takes a seat next to Mariana. After Alina's brother-in-law's defection, Mariana is one of the few fellow teachers who still speak to her.

"Some children are outright spoiled and ill-behaved. Can you imagine, after causing all that commotion with pupil Săpunaru, pupil Atanasiu didn't come to school for a week and when she did, she was completely unprepared." Alina speaks in a loud voice, so that the right persons might hear her. There are informants everywhere; she only hopes there is one in the break room now, to tell the authorities of her righteous conduct. "The cheekiness," she says, shaking her head.

Mariana covers her forearm with her hand and squeezes gently.

"What was that about? There was talk of contraband merchandise? Bubble gum, chocolates, magazines? Was she trying to sell them?" asks Mariana in a whisper.

Alina recoils. The rumors have already touched mythical proportions, but she must not try to contradict them, siding with the perpetrator. She has done herself a huge disservice by ignoring pupil Săpunaru's cries and fleeing the classroom. She replies in a booming voice, chuckling.

"Oh, no. Not that I know of. I didn't see anything, you know? I think pupil Atanasiu was just trying to get some attention."

"Oh? How come?"

"I showed her, though, what I think of such behavior. It will not be tolerated, not in my class. I gave her a four. I doubt now that pupil Atanasiu will qualify for a scholarship next semester."

*

It's the first day since the incident that Alina's heart is not racing on her way home. She has done right and also said so in the break room. The authorities will surely hear of it. There will be nothing to fear.

Her pulse settles to a regular, pleasant beat, but she still hurries her steps, by force of habit. In front of her apartment building, there is nobody waiting for her. Why should there be? She has righted the wrong.

Alina considers whether she should go to the vegetable market and buy some bell peppers to stuff while she turns the key in the great metal door. They should celebrate this relief. She pushes the apartment building door open and out of the shadow steps a man in a gray suit. He grabs her by the forearm. She tries to wrench it free, but his hold tightens.

"Comrade Mungiu? I have a few questions for you."

The Hunt

Every Tuesday afternoon, he materializes from the shadows thrown by her apartment building, from the smoke emanated by his own cigarette. He tips his hat and Alina, turning her head away from the scar severing his eyebrow in half, hastily invites him to come in. She does not want to give him time to speak, to roll those dreaded words out of some dark recess of his mind:

"Comrade, please join me at headquarters."

This sentence would be the end of her fantasy of bravery, where she plays an unknown heroine of the Resistance. In the moldy cellars of the Secret Services, she would finally deliver her pupil, between gasps and stutters, and maybe other blunt or shrill sounds she is too afraid to think of.

In her home, she can lull the Secret Service man with the warm colors in her apartment, cake, coffee, and smiles unreflected in her mismatched eyes. Mondays, she always bakes, so that the man may sit in his favorite armchair, his cigarette in one hand, the cake in the other, stretching his legs. Today, his socks are emerald green. Alina finds it easier to look at them than in his eyes, as blue as the blade of a knife, while waiting for the cut.

"Comrade, let's talk a little, eh?"

Alina nods, tracing the ash the man is littering on her handwoven carpet.

"Comrade Mungiu, on October 15th, pupil Atanasiu brought contraband items to school. I was given to understand that you facilitated the escape of the said pupil. Is that true?"

"No. My grandmother had a carpet, a piece of tapestry on the wall, did you know that? An antiquity from France, from the times before we had been enlightened by communism."

In this country, turning a blind eye is an art, a skill you must learn at a young age. Or else, the path of the snitch unravels. But he is relentless.

"Then why is the daughter of comrade Săpunaru saying that you witnessed the whole incident?"

"Ah, children fight all the time, you know? Usually, I don't pay attention. The carpet. The colors were faded, but you could still see that it was a hunt scene. In a clearing in the woods, a conglomerate of hounds, riders, beaters, all chasing a terrified deer."

Every time the Secret Service man comes, she waits for the sword above her head to fall and cut deep, but this is not his weapon of choice. He squeezes the air out of her lungs little by little, tightening her chest with menaces.

"Comrade, do you know what happens to dissidents? To their accomplices? Can you tell me, comrade?" And then, in a whisper, "You don't know, do you? Your husband—he did not tell you much, did he?"

No, Liviu didn't tell her what happened in the cellars of the Secret Services. After three days at the "headquarters," he came home smelling of piss and blood. He closed the bathroom door and let the water run for more than two hours. When he came out, he went straight to bed. Later that night, in a whim of moonlight, she saw that he had many small, round burns on the soles of his feet.

The man raises his voice while his eyes search the narrow space between her breasts, the portion of thigh he can now see. Her skirt slipped upward while she was fidgeting.

"You never wondered why he didn't tell you anything?"

"The thing always seemed a bit blown out of proportion." Her voice now quivers like her own pupils' do when reciting a poem they didn't quite learn by heart. "The hunt, I mean. All those hunters for just one deer. My grandmother had a name for that carpet. *La chasse*? No, that's not it. I can't—"

"Comrade, you are being uncooperative. You are misleading me on purpose. I asked a simple question."

"No, no, I didn't see anything! Why don't you believe me?"

She's shrill and teary eyed. He grabs her trembling hand.

"I want you to think carefully until next week. Maybe you'll remember something."

Letting her go, he rises to leave, but their fingers touch when she hands him his coat and his nose brushes her hair when he leans to take his hat. Their shoulders graze as he makes his way to the door. Alina knows that if she screams, nobody will hear her.

"It's *battue*," he says without turning.

"Excuse me?"

They're standing in the narrow hallway and his manly odors make something within her constrict.

"That word you were seeking. It's *battue*."

"Of course. *Battue*. Beaten."

The Pinch

Sometimes, Liviu pinches her buttocks when she stoops to gather the empty plates. He grabs her flesh between his fingers, twists, and pulls. He says he means it as a joke, but the clenching of his jaws says the opposite.

Tonight, he catches her by surprise, and she drops a plate to the floor. While she is sweeping the shards, he says, "Be careful next time! We don't have enough money to replace everything you break."

The plate belongs to a set of six they received as a wedding gift from Aunt Theresa. The plate is now a metaphor for something—Alina can find plenty of examples in her life to compare it to.

Disenchantment

I choose to visit Aunt Theresa on a Monday—I know who I will find there. But I'm late. As I come in, the two nuns are leaving. They're both tall and probably lean. I can't tell because of their ample black robes. They have wrinkled, pale faces and hands with long, thin fingers. Their skin has a translucence that captures light like an aura, probably from all the praying. The nuns come to town every Monday to buy flour and oil and whatever they can't craft or grow themselves. They always come by my aunt Theresa's and she slips them a few bars of Fa soap or a bag of Tide detergent. When I was a schoolgirl, I read that in the Middle Ages the rich bought the absolution of their sins with gold. I wonder if this is what she is doing— buying herself clemency for what she does every third Wednesday of each month.

Aunt Theresa squeezes their hands, as if she's kneading their essence between her own bony fingers. The nuns leave behind an aroma of frankincense, wax, and cleanliness. I want to run after them, bury my head in their chests, allow them to soothe me. Instead, I take off my boots. By the time I enter the living room, my heart is thumping again.

"Alina? Are you feeling all right?" asks my aunt.

I collapse in an armchair, stare at my own knees. I feel the sturdy frame of my aunt settling on the armrest. I take her hand, the one that had touched the nuns, hoping that something good will rub off it.

"I barely sleep at night," I say. "I barely eat. In fact, I barely do anything besides obsessing whether they'll arrest me or not."

"Arrest you? Who would arrest you?" she says, drawing her hand away.

I bury my face in my palms and tell her everything in a single breath: about the children, the magazine, the man with a scar above his left eye. I tell her about his hungry looks, the way he repeats the same questions, the unspoken threat of the "headquarters." I tell her things that I do not dare tell my husband. I only look at her when I am done. She shakes her head, but her bracelets are silent.

"This is disgusting," she says. "All of this—just because children were being children."

She opens a window, wrenches a cigarette free from its package. She strikes the lighter three times before she manages to conjure a flame.

"Sometimes I think there is something deeply wrong with this country."

"Can you help me?" I ask.

"Help you? Of course I can. I suspect someone has done charms on you. Could you come next

Wednesday? I'm expecting two gypsy witches and a fortune teller. Sure. We'll see what we can do for you."

When I was eleven years old, a witch woman stopped me on the street and asked me for a bank-note. Startled, I gave her the five-lé* bill I was meant to buy bread with. She folded it, made a few quick movements with her hands, and puff! The bill was gone. Then she said that if I screamed, if I asked the other people on the street for help, the devil would come and steal me. I returned home crying, with no bread. When I told my mother, she took out my fa-ther's leather belt. I remember that my bottom still burned at dinner. Much later, in high school, when all my friends went to have their futures told, I re-fused to join them.

"I don't want to have anything to do with witches. How about cousin Matei? He works for the Secret Services, doesn't he?"

She snorts smoke out of her nostrils—the extin-guished fire of a dragon.

"That's *precisely* why he can't do anything for you. What credibility would he have afterward?"

I grind my teeth. "Really, you too?"

"My dear, it's bad enough for us that your brother-in-law is a defector. Matei can't intercede on your behalf. But I could say an incantation against the evil eye."

* *Romanian currency.*

By the time she returns with a bowl of water and a matchbox, I'm already in the hallway, putting on my boots. She lifts her fingers to make the sign of the cross, but I turn my back and slam the door. On the way home, all I can think about is calling my mother. When we're scared, we all cry for our mothers.

Slip

Liviu's chomping and crunching drives Alina away from the table, making her throw her half-full plate in the sink. It clashes with a hollow sound. She turns up the water and begins to wash the dishes, to cover his noises. He doesn't even lift his head.

Last year, they needed two tables to accommodate their eleven guests: their own, and a borrowed one from the neighbors. The tables sagged with the weight of the food: Russian and Asian salads, smoked sausages and pastramis, homemade noodle soup, roast beef and stuffed pork.

Today, only a few distant friends, who hadn't heard about her brother-in-law's defection, called to overflow her with dry congratulations. Not even her mother is there—she's in Eforie, for a health cure.

Alina wants them to flee for the evening, to a restaurant, but when Liviu returns from work, it's already too late and he is tired. He doesn't even notice her elegant dark-blue dress, her new earrings, or her red lipstick, clotted on her lips from waiting. There is nothing left for her other than to conjure a quick meal out of the leftovers of yesterday's pork steak.

Alina wishes for nothing more than to be able to run from themselves for one day, from this evening like any other, this air between them as they sit face-to-face at the living room table, thick with the alcohol vapors Liviu exhales. Everybody drinks on the commute, and Liviu has plenty of time to do so, to "fraternize" with the other workers on the train. What faster road to friendship is there than the one slippery with cheap vodka? It is the end of the world where he is going, and when he returns, he is always tired, and his weariness makes everything around them wither and wilt.

Liviu kisses her on the cheek, a wary lover, a less-than-dutiful husband. Once he closes the bedroom door, she cuts herself a lonely slice of birthday cake. It's strawberries and buttercream, her favorite. She places it on the kitchen table and lights herself a cigarette. Alina is accustomed to this exhaling of smoke in the air filled only with silence, in the quiet breaks in the teacher's room, in the afternoon hours, which are lately dilating and throwing longer shadows.

Liviu's plate lingers on the table, an unwanted presence. Alina puts out her cigarette in the leftover mashed potatoes and takes out the cake from the fridge. She tilts it over the garbage bin, so that it slips soundlessly in.

Of Gifts of Unknown Provenance

It looks excitingly modern. Its keys are white, except for the first one in the second row, which is red. I turn the round black handle and the cold plastic sends shivers down my spine and at the same time ignites a warm feeling in the depths of my stomach. Yes. This is how I will roll them out. Then I will pile them up and climb one piece of paper at a time toward my dream.

In the other corner of the table, my mother is arranging her fur hat, smiling. The self-sufficiency I read on her face reminds me I should take everything that comes from her with a grain of salt. Up until now, dealing with her was like dealing with the devil—the costs always surpassed the benefits, like comparing Everest with a molehill.

I had buried my dream and mourned it properly a month ago, when Rodica from Bucharest told me over the telephone, in her obnoxiously nasal voice, that she would not be needing me to contribute to the math exercise book anymore. I stared at the hand-written pages of exercises for hours and hours in a row through my clouded eyes, wishing to be able to destroy them. Their sight was a constant reminder of my failures.

"There," my mother says. "Now you can write your *own* exercise book. You don't need to share that first page with anyone." She leans toward me, winking. "You know what you could afford from the royalties you would receive from the book? Lawyers."

"Why would I want a lawyer?" I quip, pretending not to understand. "Thank you. This is a gift from Heaven." I stroke my typewriter like a favorite cat.

My mother fumbles in her purse and draws out a cigarette. She blows the smoke toward Liviu's jacket, forgotten on one of the dining room chairs.

"Sweetie. You look more pleased and happy now than you ever have since you married that peasant of yours."

The glowing tip of her cigarette draws a circle around my head. I could reply that it's not my husband's fault that I'm not happy, but her own refusal to support me, forcing me into taking a job I never liked. My hand on the typewriter feels awfully cold—strange enough, for a gift from hell. Not strange at all, considering the fact that she wields this gift like a dagger, hoping to slash a rift of separation between me and my husband. I could say something about her attempt at manipulation. Instead, I tell her, "I'm delighted by your present!"

She smiles. "And don't pretend you don't understand what I mean about the lawyers."

If she only knew how close Liviu and I dance on the verge of divorce, and how he doesn't need her help to pirouette away from me. How much more smug could that smile of hers be?

She pats my knee, like one would stroke an obedient dog. "But the two of us, we always understood each other, didn't we?"

I glance again at the typewriter, at the metallic glare of the keys, its weight on my table, sealing a pact. And to think that my mother is the one who taught me never to accept gifts of unknown provenance.

The Skirt

The year when the Beloved Leader came to our town, my mother didn't cook us dinner for eleven days in a row. The Beloved Leader had to inaugurate a truck factory, and my mother was tailoring a skirt from dark-red tweed.

The skirt was meant to be tight at the top and flaring at the bottom, ending at knee level. Something must have gone wrong, because my mother had to undo it after six days and start again. After that, she barely spoke to me. She went around the house with the measuring tape draped around her neck like a necklace, pins stuck in her collar.

The day after the skirt was done, my teacher came to school wearing it. The folds had a liquid quality about them, shifting with every motion. Two days later, on the day that the nominations for the position of flower bearer were made, my teacher was wearing the skirt again. When the moment came, she called my name and my classmates applauded. It was the greatest honor imaginable: coming close to the Beloved Leader, giving him flowers.

At home, my mother and I practiced the act of bestowing.

A week later, a lady with a purple hat came from the Party to inspect all candidates. The nominees were rounded up in the school festivity hall.

We went up on stage in groups of six, where she would ask us to smile, turn, walk, and pretend that we were giving flowers. When it was my turn to perform, she leaned in closer. She smelled of tobacco, coffee, and a Bulgarian rose perfume my aunt also used to wear. She asked me if my eyes were mismatched. I informed her that I had a gray eye and a brown eye.

The lady wrinkled her nose. It didn't occur to me to explain that there were many mismatched things in my life. For instance, my mother's expectations.

My mother asked me how it went. When I told her, her lips tightened as if a magic string had been pulled through their flesh and someone was tugging hard at it.

That spring, the Beloved Leader came, and I was not there to give him flowers.

For the remainder of the school year, we dined in silence and I didn't lift my offending eyes from the plate.

Quotes from My Mother (Commented)—Part II

"Did you know that Alexandra split up with her . . . friend and is now living with her mother?" Wistful look, puppy eyes. "She probably will, for the rest of her life. Who would want to marry her now, after such a scandal?"

Alexandra was my childhood friend, the daughter of our neighbors. Before my own life fell apart, she ran away with a married man and was the talk of the town for two months. But then, the married man did what married men do, which is go home to their wives. *Divorce* is another word the communist authorities don't like.

To my mother, my friend's broken heart is not the point of the story. Nor does she take a moralistic or religious point of view, on the line of, "She got what she deserved" (to her own credit, like most of her friends do). For her, the point is that Alexandra's mother will now have a companion slash person to be talked to and talked at, slash to cook, slash to nurse her in the final years of her life. She envies Alexandra's mother.

But, on the other hand, my mother is right. If my friend doesn't move away from here, chances are that she'll never find another man. It's a small town. People do little but talk.

"If anything bad happens between you and your husband, you could come live with me."

I cut her short with an "I know, Mom," dismissing her idea, but the truth is that I've actually been thinking about it.

I can see no point in sharing a bed with Liviu if all I do is turn my back to him, wincing at his smell of alcohol. No point in our dinners together if the silence is broken only by my forced chirps nobody listens to, punctuated by my husband's complaints. No point in the pecks on the cheek we call "kisses" that we still give to each other because that is expected from a married couple.

Sundays are the hardest days of the week. I can't wait for the day to end, to wake up on Monday morning, to put my makeup on and go to school. I can hardly wait for the weight of the day we spent as a couple to lift slowly from my shoulders, like steam rising from cooling water.

On Sunday, few sounds break the shroud of silence between us: the typewriter burning letters and numbers in black ink on a sheet of paper, and the rustling of a book ruffled by my husband. But these notes are too weak to slash this covering open, they only puncture holes in it, just enough to allow me to breathe. Sometimes, I'm not typing my exercises at all, I just keep striking the keys so that Liviu won't raise his eyes and ask, "So, we're not doing anything today, either? You never do anything but write, anyway."

These are the times when I think of what we were before Mihai's defection. Of who Liviu was—a man I would never, ever have thought of leaving.

"So, have you finished your book?"

Yes, I have, but I'm having so much trouble placing it. It seems I can't do anything without the right connections and I am notorious for all the wrong ones. Not even the smaller presses will consider my manuscript. Fortunately, I have a plan that involves the Head School Inspector of our county.

However, I tell none of the above to my mother. I say, "I need to make a few minor adjustments before it is finished."

I don't enjoy lying to her, but she has such a bad habit of using all the rejections I have ever received like a hot poker glowing white, twisting it in my open wounds.

"I never asked you this, but when you were in trouble, did you call your aunt?"

Yes, I did, and I even paid her a visit. She invited me to her place, and there were no nuns, no fortune tellers, no other friends of hers. She told me, toying with her bracelets, spinning them around her tiny wrists as if looking for the angle in the ellipse that catches the most light, "Matei got wind at work about a colleague of his, Victor, paying you regular visits. He told this man that you are his cousin and that he is particularly fond of you. I expect this is the last you will ever see of him."

My grin was so wide that my cheeks were aching.

"Matei asked me if I knew, and I told him I did. He said I should have told him. I'm sorry," she said. "I can be such an old bat sometimes. I'm sorry."

I try to blame her for the way she behaved, but I can't. I can't blame a bitch for growling and barking and biting anyone who comes near her fresh litter of puppies. There are things in us, older than conscience, or the acquiescence of God, instincts we can't control, no matter how hard we try to pull their reins. But I often ask myself, if Aunt Theresa is protecting her pups, then who is my mother safe-guarding?

For Sale

Alina and Corina, the inspector's secretary, exchange strained smiles again. Alina avoids looking at her; she doesn't want to make the woman feel under pressure. It's not her fault that the inspector takes his time and that she has been waiting for almost two hours. Corina has already delivered. In exchange for Jacobs coffee and Dominican cocoa she set this appointment, made it possible for Alina to sit in the inspector's antechamber, heart thumping, praying for her last chance not to be wasted.

Alina would stare into the manuscript in her lap, but her eyes are foggy from looking at its first page, the paper curled and damp under her sweaty palms.

The grandfather clock in the antechamber strikes three.

*

The inspector hasn't lifted his gaze once in the ten minutes Alina has been in his office. His pen scratches a piece of blotted paper.

"Comrade Mungiu? Did you come here to stare while I make my notes?"

"No, comrade Inspector."

The inspector has a black spot on his lower lip, where his cigarette usually hangs. The tips of his fingers are as yellow as the cover of the file he is reading.

"Comrade Mungiu, I am a very busy man. My secretary keeps squeezing people in, though I have to finish these assessments by Monday. But since you're already here, by all means, speak!"

Alina places the manuscript on the inspector's packed desk.

"Comrade Inspector . . . Last year I began writing a math exercises book, with comrades Rodica Ionescu and Vasilica Popa, from Bucharest. In May, when I telephoned with comrade Ionescu, she told me that they no longer needed my collaboration and—"

"Get to the point."

"I already had a lot of exercises, comrade Inspector, and they are very good. I've managed to place about a dozen with math journals throughout the—"

"Comrade Mungiu, you are wasting my time. Congratulations for placing your exercises successfully."

The inspector rises from his seat, stretching his hand to shake Alina's. It's the first time they look into each other's eyes, and he makes that searching, disbelieving face all people do when confronted with her mismatched eyes. Alina pushes the manuscript in front of his nose. *Alina Mungiu. Math Exercise Book for I–IV Grade*, says the title.

"The book. It's done. I've written my own book. Please. You're my last chance."

When Alina was in elementary school, children had to coat their handbooks in transparent covers and stick labels with their names on top of them. Alina always placed her label above the authors' names. Sometimes, during class, she looked at the first page and admired the names. She still knows them all by heart: Serdean, Romanian, second grade; Constantinescu, History, fourth grade; Almas and Fotescu, Grammar, third grade; and so on.

The inspector pushes the manuscript away from him.

"Comrade Mungiu, you're wasting my time."

"Please." Her voice quivers like a strung arrow. "I called all the possible presses, and Ursu Press told me that, if you approve of the manuscript, they'll print a small edition. Please. Just read it, it's not much—"

The inspector pushes the manuscript away with two fingers. The first page is slipping slowly from the top.

Alina almost gave up when Rodica told her she was no longer interested in their collaboration, but then her mother bought her the typewriter, a few days after her birthday.

Since then, she's been scribbling ideas in the

breaks or even during class at school, typing until late at night, looking at unfinished exercises while stirring the contents of one pot or another.

"Comrade Inspector . . . Please . . . It's very good, I assure you. If you could just take a look at it, I promise."

The inspector lifts the receiver. "Corina? Please tell my next appointment to come in."

"Comrade Inspector! The press. They said—"

"Maybe the press doesn't know who you are. I do."

The inspector pushes the manuscript toward Alina with the tips of his fingers, afraid to soil himself. The manuscript falls on the floor, scattering.

"Comrade Mungiu! There is no need for hysterics, for throwing papers on the floor!"

When the inspector wrinkles his nose, like he does now, his black spot dilates, threatening to spill and smear her, too.

Alina bends and gathers the scattered pages. They are worth less than toilet paper.

On her way home, Alina stops by the local newspaper and scribbles an announcement. "Used typewriter for sale."

Reel

3. How It Ends

The Secret Service man, her Victor, places a finger under Alina's chin, lifting her head. She looks full into the headlights of his eyes. The smile that illuminates them comes from his whip-wielding, foot-stomping, flesh-tearing depths.

"So? What would you prefer, my dear comrade Mungiu?"

Alina's hands dangle on the side of her body like the hands of a hanged woman. "I do hope you'll pay me a visit next Tuesday. I'll be expecting you eagerly for our weekly chat. Do you prefer a certain kind of cake?"

The Secret Service man chuckles and opens the door. "We'll see."

Alina moves to follow him, to pull him back, to tell him she'd give him anything he wants. From the threshold, she notices that all her fellow teachers are grouped in front of the door. She's rooted.

In the hallway, the bustle of pupils running on polished concrete fades as the two men walk toward the exit. Children scurry back into their classrooms, even though the break has just begun.

The other teachers slip by her into the break room. They sip their cold coffees in silence, their faces like cassettes with their tape pulled out, unwinding every bit of conversation they had with her in the past few years.

Thursday morning, Miss Puiu bars her entrance to the break room. She tells Alina, "We thought you might enjoy your coffee more in your own classroom."

Alina receives a steaming cup she can't grab by the handle, wrapping her hand around the container. The heat makes her fingers jittery, and she drops the cup. Coffee splashes on Alina's shoes, her pantyhose, her coat. Alina kicks the shards, steps into her classroom. Sharp fragments lie in the hallway all day long like a poisonous snake nobody wants to touch.

2. That Endless Middle

The other man from the Secret Services, the bald one with his red nose and puffy hands, keeps asking questions: sharp, unyielding like so many knives chopping through her flesh.

"So you're insinuating that pupil Săpunaru is a liar? That the daughter of the Chief of Police is a fabricator?"

An oniony smell from her own sticky armpits drifts toward Alina. "No, no, no. It's just that she misinterpreted the situation. It didn't happen as you think, as she thinks it did. She saw. She—"

"I believe that a cross-interrogation with the other witnesses is necessary. What do you think?" says the bald man, glancing at Victor, who's leaning back in his chair with his arms crossed.

Victor shrugs. Since their arrival, he's been as silent as a piece of furniture. He just glares at Alina, occasionally touching her under the table with the tip of his shoe.

"No, no!" says Alina. "Not the children, not an interrogation, not at their age! Don't you realize, they'll have nightmares for weeks!"

"Nightmares?" asks the bald man. "Why would they have nightmares? Would they have anything to hide? I say, we interrogate them here, or at Headquarters next week. Of course, I could leave this entire affair to my esteemed colleague."

Victor pushes the sole of his rubber shoe into Alina's shin. She wants to pull her leg away, but the chair allows her to move only so much. She has no escape; she has to endure.

"I prefer not to find myself alone with comrade Mungiu any longer," says Victor. "There have been some complaints regarding my treatment of her."

"No, no," she says. "It's all a misunderstanding. Someone misunderstood."

The bald Secret Service man slams the file in front of him shut. "We have to go. We'll agree on the further proceedings in the car, esteemed colleague."

The men rise to their feet, and so does Alina, in spite of the sharp pain in her calf where Victor's shoe nested. The bald man walks ahead, Victor lags behind. He stops on the threshold, waiting for her to catch up.

1. The Auspicious Beginning

This Tuesday, Alina's Secret Service man, Victor, doesn't arrive. She waits for him until five, then gets out and buys whipped-cream-and-strawberry diplomat cake to celebrate. It's delicious, and Alina has a sweet tooth today, so she even eats Liviu's portion. She hides the smudged paper trail deep within the garbage can.

On Wednesday, Alina is sipping her tea in the teachers' break room when someone knocks on the door. Miss Puiu moves aside to let in two men with felt hats and long, dark coats. One of them is Victor. The other one is a bald man with a red nose. *Poor soul they're after*, thinks Alina.

"Comrade Mungiu?" says the bald man.

Alina looks around. She sees raised eyebrows, wide eyes, puckered mouths: the expression of so many alterations in her colleagues' perception of her. The break room will never be the same again.

Alina wonders if this is about her husband. The teachers step out of the room. The bald man spreads his yellow file, as thick as a layered cake, on the table. He has to push aside dirty cups, half-filled with coffee. Victor seats himself and leans back in his chair. His body posture is relaxed—he seems to be at home anywhere she is.

The bald man asks, "Comrade Mungiu, did you witness pupil Atanasiu bringing contraband items to school last year?"

Alina stares into her nearly empty cup. The coffee grounds have arranged themselves in a pattern like angel wings, but dark. If she had been as skilled in reading the signs as her aunt, perhaps she would have been able to divine her fall.

The Pinch—Take Two

Tonight, Liviu pinches her buttocks again, when she stoops to gather the plates. He grabs her flesh between his fingers, twists, and pulls, clenching his jaws.

Tonight, Alina slaps him. Liviu jumps up from his seat.

"Are you crazy?"

"Don't you touch me again!" she screams.

He grabs her wrist. She jerks away, takes one of the plates from the table, and smashes it on the floor. Liviu jumps again, this time to avoid the angry shards coming for his shins.

"*Are you crazy?* Those were a wedding gift!"

"I'm so tired of this! Of you, of this, of you!"

She grabs the second plate and flings it at the wall, like a Frisbee. Liviu cowers and covers his face.

"Stop it!"

"You stop it! Stop complaining and getting drunk but most of all, stop fucking pinching me!" she screeches. "*I want out!*"

*

Now Alina's crying, face in her palms, blood dripping from the back of her hand. Liviu tiptoes between the shards and touches her shoulder.

He says, "I want our life back, too."

"There is no going back, but we can't live like this, either." She uncovers her face, glares at him. When Liviu looks like he does now, his eyes a wet blue from all the tears he is holding back, his hair ruffled like the fur of a dog who has just gotten into a fight, Alina can't imagine that she ever thought of deserting him.

"No, we can't live like this," he says, and Alina wonders if he sometimes thinks of leaving her, too.

She wants to get up and embrace him so hard until the possibility of them ever parting is squeezed out of their beings, until their skins melt into each other, the love-life equivalent of a bomb with cold fusion. But his hand on her shoulder pins her down and she cowers in herself, her core turning into something tiny and evil. She wants to confess her small betrayals, her thoughts of abandoning him, like a sinner asking for absolution, when Liviu says, "I've been thinking of something lately. But it might be dangerous."

Alina wipes a thread of snot with the sleeve of her dress and pushes his hand aside. She vanishes into the living room, and just as Liviu asks, "What's wrong?" she returns with the radio.

She places it on the kitchen counter and turns the volume up as loud as possible. It's an old folk song about migratory herding and missing home. Alina leans close to Liviu's ear.

"I didn't have the chance to tell you, but Aunt Theresa gave me an idea the last time I saw her. It's been on my mind ever since. And now that you're mentioning it, we might be actually thinking about the same thing."

A Comprehensive but Not Exhaustive List of Reasons for Asking for an Italian Visa

1. "We're trying to escape from this godforsaken country."

Though the truest of them all, nay, the only reason we want a visa, I doubt it would be a very good idea to tell this to the bureaucrats at the Italian embassy. Of course, we could play the pity card, but I'm not sure it would work. Plus, I'm sure that the Romanian Secret Services have ears there, too, and we wouldn't want them to hear that we're trying to defect.

"No, no, no, this just won't do," says Liviu, leaning toward me.

I ruffle his short blond hair, and he smiles. The radio is turned up so loud that I'm sure my neighbors from the ground floor can hear the wary commentator praise the peasants of Flăcărica for their production of grapes this year, covering the smooth bubbling of the tripe soup on the stove. As I tell him about my idea, my nose is in my husband's ear. He smells of vervain soap and old books. I kiss the tip of his lobe and he chuckles.

We first wanted to go to Germany—as we both speak the language—but because it's so close to France and my brother-in-law Mihai, I doubt that Border Control will allow us to leave the country, even if we obtain the visas. Using a geography manual for fifth graders, we decided on Italy.

In our fantasies, whispered in a low voice when we think nobody might be listening, Liviu's face has new dimensions, conjured by the Italian sun. There's a playful gleam starting in the corner of his eyes, wrinkled by the crooked smiles that remind me of the boy I met at Constanţa. It's with this boy that I drink an espresso so oily and stiff that I'm afraid to stir it with my teaspoon, for fear that it might blow us up with the flavor. It's this boy's hand I hold as I stroll down a hallway in the Uffizi, and as I cross the Roman Forum. Which leads me to the next idea.

2. "We're going on a vacation. We'd like to visit Rome, and Ravenna, and Venice, and Milan, and Florence. Especially Florence."

This could work. Who wouldn't like to vacation in Italy? The essence of lives lived long ago seeping through stones like the sweat of palms that laid them one on top of the other. The bodies those hands belonged to, eons ago turned to an amorphous mass of ash, prettier than what we'd become once the breath has gone from our shells of flesh. Another reason to want to live the *dolce vita* in the present.

Liviu nibbles at a pink fudge cookie. "Traveling to the West for pleasure, with a brother who's a defector?" He shakes his head. "We need something else. Something more serious."

"Like what?"

I get up from my seat and stir the tripe soup. It's almost ready. I head to the fridge to pick out two eggs and sour cream, for the finishing touches. As I walk across the kitchen, I lean my ear toward Liviu's lips, to hear what he has to say.

"Something scientific. Something designed to flatter the Party and the Regime. They might let us go, if they think we're working for the fame and glory of the Motherland."

I fold the egg into the sour cream, then add hot soup to the mixture, a spoonful at a time, stirring, careful not to make the yolk clot. A tiny mistake, and my work of four hours would be ruined. I hold my breath. Liviu steps to my side, wraps his hand around my waist.

3. "We're writing a research paper on Roman influences in architecture in the Carpatho-Danubian space in the third century AD."

My hand holding the bowl freezes midair. "You can't possibly have come up with this just now."

He rubs his nose in my ear.

"Isn't it just brilliant? Using my history studies, my passion for archaeology, to write a research paper that would show the extent of Roman influences in the space that later became Romania. Or—even better—vice versa. Taking examples of Dacian architecture, how they were implemented in Rome. And you're helping me with the documentation."

He speaks quicker, and louder. He fidgets behind me. His own idea is sweeping him away. I nudge him, careful not to spill the contents of my bowl.

"But there is none," I reply. "Dacians built in wood, there might as well be nothing left."

He blows in my soup. "You never learn, do you? Historical accuracy is of no consequence to the Government. It says whatever it likes—and it has to be true. It glorifies those who make it add up. By the way, I think your soup is still too hot for eggs."

I ponder.

4. "We're writing this research paper, and we have to compare Roman architecture across Italy and Germany. This way, we show how Dacian culture was exported to the fringes of the Roman Empire."

He chuckles. "Clever, clever. But why?"

"Don't you see?" I say. "We have two attempts at obtaining a visa this way. Doubles our chances."

He holds me tight, burrows his nose in my hair. "Rosewater," he says. "You smell of rosewater. And your plan is magnificent."

I drop the contents of the bowl into the cooking pot, stirring. Underneath, the yellowish mass of soup becomes white and silky. There aren't any clots.

I say, "It's perfect."

What We Had to Give Away So That We Could Buy a Fourteen-Year-Old Dacia So That We Would Have an Independent Means of Transportation in Order to Flee the Country

What We Had to Give	To Whom
Liviu's share of his mother's plum orchard	To a neighbor who produces impressive quantities of schnapps every year, using the said plums and a distiller he usually hides in a cheese barrel
The gold earrings that belonged to my grandmother	To Aunt Theresa, who gave me ten times their value for them
Liviu's collection of rare stamps	To an eleven-year-old whose mother is one of the Chief Secretaries of the Party
The manuscript for the math exercise book	To Rodica from Bucharest after bargaining worse than two fishwives on a market day
Our wedding rings	To a tractor driver from Seceratu

Like Music

There's something in the way we swirl around each other late in the evening, whispering in each other's ears, gathering the remnants of our feast. There's something in the way we smile and hold hands, turn the TV, radio, up loud, leave the water running, confounding the men who tapped into our lives, so we can speak and make plans about our brightening future. There's something in the way hope creeps up behind our backs and presses its palms against our eyes, leaving us smiling, but blind to the future. And we are both reluctant to speak its name, for fear that it might vanish. There's something in the way we hold each other at night, like shipwrecked passengers, like that summer when the sea was licking at our toes, like the first time we met. There's something in the way we say, *We will, We will, We will,* ringing in our ears like music.

Paparudă

It's the week after Easter, and I'm in a car. You'd think
Liviu and I would be gliding toward the border—
West Germany approved our visa last week—but
instead, he decided to wait for the Italian one, too.
So, I'm in Aunt Theresa's car again, meandering on
a country path that defies the logic that roads should
take the shortest course between two points.

Today, Aunt Theresa called and asked for my
help. "There's a drought," she told me. We needed
her help, too, so I couldn't deny her a favor. Here I
am in her Volga, listening to her telling me how this
is the old wagon road that once delineated the border between the peasants' lands and the estate of the
boieri*—our ancestors.

"When the company came to build the road in the
1930s," she says, "they offered sums for the patches
of land they needed for the road that made your head
spin, and yet your grandfather refused to sell. Back

---

* *Member of the Romanian nobility.*

then, he said he had a moral duty to his forefathers to pass on the estate untouched. If only he knew!"

When the communists came to power, they took everything from him and would have claimed his life too, if my grandmother hadn't shrunk him. This was years before I was born. I grew up in the reassuringly sterile concrete environment of a newly built ten-story apartment building. The musty smell of wet earth, the spikes of wheat in my palms, the leathery faces of peasants say nothing to me, unlike Aunt Theresa, whom the villagers always call in their hour of need.

I have my needs too: the need to tell her about the visa, the need for sound advice. But breaking this silence would be like crushing a crystal glass under my foot. Aunt Theresa steers into the village, while dirty, barefooted children wave at her. She drives on, to the old house, the *boieri*'s mansion. In front of it, dozens of men and women in traditional costumes, dark wool skirts and trousers, and *ii*—white shirts embroidered in blue—are waiting for us. The women hold crowns and garlands made of woven leaves and branches decorated with red ribbons. An old woman with a dark head-kerchief, wrinkled as time itself, steps up to Aunt Theresa and kisses her on the cheek. Aunt Theresa grabs her hand, squeezes it hard. She then turns to me.

"Alina, take off your clothes."

*

You'd think that the rain has come, a fearful storm, if you listened to the claps of the hands, the snap of fingers, the wooden spoons drumming into cauldrons, but the dust, this dry dust rises to my thighs, barely licking my belly, an indecent lover aroused by the fact that the entire village is watching us, singing:

Paparudă, rudă,
vino de ne udă—*

And they sing faster, faster, faster, and my feet are spinning, and I have no power over them as I leap and jump, making the dust rise higher and higher, caressing my breasts, and two old women pour buckets of water over us, making my dust hiss and rise one more time, caressing me, becoming one with me as its breath dies, and Aunt Theresa is right behind me, jingling jade beads and chanting an incantation, words I can't make out, in a low voice, like a rumble of thunder, and the song of the villagers goes on, even as we pass the church and the men and women cross themselves, but I can't, because my hands move to the music, the makeshift sounds of rain, and so do my bare feet, waking the dust, helping it insinuate under my skirt made of leaves and weeds, I have nothing under it, nothing on my torso except for a garland of leaves on my breasts which the men watch as they bob and dangle with my jumps, my nipples hardening be-

* Paparudă, ruda/come and wet us.

cause of the cold water being poured on me, or maybe it's the touch of dust. Oh, let me taste you, roll in you, in our embrace, before the rain comes and extinguishes you.

*

On our way back, in the car, I catch my breath. My cheeks burn with the shame of having been seen naked by the entire village. I sniff. In this blinding afternoon light, the darkest thoughts are flooding my mind: *I paraded naked in front of dozens of people—the shame! We'll be trapped in Romania forever. We'll wait for the Italian visa until the German one expires.*

I'd love to speak to Aunt Theresa, but I'm too angry because of what she made me do.

She places a hand over mine and says, "You've done well, you've helped a lot."

"Bullshit."

She turns to me, startled, and shakes her head. "You don't even know how much good you've done. But make sure you lie with your husband tonight. Or else, you're marked."

"Marked for what?" I say.

"The Paparudă is an ancient ritual, meant to bring the rain," she says. "It's a fertility ritual. Lie with your husband."

I wrench my hand away.

At home, I crash onto my bed, fall into a deep sleep. In my dream, the dust arranges itself in Victor's face, and his fingers are grabbing me, tearing, pinching, caressing, and the villagers drum their song of rain. I open my eyes. It's the middle of the night, and Liviu is fast asleep beside me. A drumming on glass summons me to the window. I walk toward it, still pregnant with sleep, and peer outside. It's raining.

Typewriter Money

"What in the name of God have you been telling your mother?" asks Aunt Theresa when she opens the door.

I dance over the threshold, pivot around her to the hallway, take off my shoes. The cold tiles soothe my dilated feet.

"Outside, the air burns your lungs if you try to breathe in," I say. "She called you, I assume?"

Aunt Theresa smirks. "She asked me to stop telling you nonsense. Garbage. Would you like some tea? Coffee?"

"Water from the fridge."

I plunked two cubes of sugar in my coffee and watched them sink and dissolve.

"Why do you want to know about my cousins?" asked my mother. "I haven't had any contact with them since before you were born."

"Aunt Theresa said that they fled to France first, but then settled somewhere in Germany. That they had been granted political asylum."

"What is with all these questions? Has Aunt

Theresa contacted them? If that is the case, it is our duty to report her."

"Of course," I said, sipping my coffee. It scalded, conjuring tiny blisters on my tongue. I brushed the newly sprouted bumps against my lips. "I was just wondering."

"Do you want more trouble with the Secret Services than you already have?" she asked. She leaned toward me, whispered in my ear. "This could endanger your book, do you realize? Especially now that it's going so well! Do you have any news?"

In the living room: a green cylinder with a zipper, made of impermeable cloth, almost as tall as me. I shriek.

"You did it, didn't you? How did you manage? Was it witchcraft again?" I tease.

"Ha!" she chuckles. "Not this time. I asked one of the managers of the universal store to call around. They found one in Sibiu. They shipped it with an ambulance."

I finger the zipper, feeling the cloth my new tent is made of.

"An ambulance? Why an ambulance?"

Aunt Theresa waves, clinking her bracelets. "Don't ask."

"Is it normal that I'm still horrified about how things can be arranged in this country?"

"It should please you," she says. "This is the place where everything is possible."

"Or *impossible*," I correct her. "It depends on if you're on the good side of the authorities or not."

"Yup," I said, stirring in my cup. "The inspector sent the manuscript to Bucharest for reviewing. He told me not to tell anyone, but it looks good."

My mother smirked, patted my leg.

"There you go!" She brushed her hand through my hair. "I'm so proud of you!"

I wanted to tell her about the inspector. I swear. But then I had to ask about my cousins and it would have been too much, all of a sudden. It's been more than a month since my appointment, since it turned out my manuscript is worth no more than the paper it is written on. Perhaps good enough to start a fire.

But the last time the two of us met I was too tired—I had to rehearse with the children for the winter festivities, and one of the girls kept forgetting her lines, so we had to start from the beginning over and over again. And the time before that my mother was upset because she couldn't find a full gas cylinder in the whole town. So there seemed to be no breaking of this circle of lies, and I was compelled to ask, "Is it true that you had a governess? That you wrote poems in French when you were a teenager? That you had a piano, and not the upright kind, in your house?"

Batting my eyelashes, tilting my head, avoiding the blow long before my mother thought of administering it.

"Really, Alina. Can't we converse on other subjects? You know that I don't like to talk about my family."

"The typewriter is so nice," I said. "It's a pity

not to use it. I was thinking about writing about our family history."

"I don't think that our family history agrees with the principles of Socialism, though."

The old cliché "attack is the best defense" seems to be true. I don't want her to ask about the typewriter and she doesn't.

"The cousin of one of our coworkers has lent us a guide to all the camping places in Austria. I don't have anything for Germany, though," I say.

"Don't worry. You'll find something once you're there. You can look for your uncles in Nuremberg. And you can always sleep in the car."

I caress the coarse sackcloth.

"I can't believe this. I can't believe we're so close to doing this." I get up, extracting an envelope from my white purse. "Tell me how much the tent costs."

"Don't worry, you can pay me later. Besides, it's Monday. Do you want to be giving money the whole week?"

I clack my tongue.

"Oh, please. I really want to do this," I say. "I have the typewriter money."

Aunt Theresa cocks an eyebrow.

"I finally found a buyer."

One of these days, I'll tell my mother everything. About the inspector, the typewriter, our plans to escape. I will. I just have to find the perfect moment. And when I do, I will confess it all. She is bound to do what all mothers do: be happy if I am happy, even if this entails staying with Liviu, turning our backs on our country. This is what mothers do.

Aunt Theresa throws me a long glance before she closes the door.

"Be careful with your mother," she says. Sometimes I think that she can read my thoughts, but only when I don't want her to. "You never know what to expect from her. I certainly hope she doesn't suspect anything."

Cutting Short

Today, even the wind thwarts me. It's so hard to keep the flame burning on my father's grave. I try to shelter the slender wax candle in a tin box that once served as a container for powdered milk. I snap a flame into life and bend the lighter toward the already scorched string of the candle. The wind swells again, makes the fire pinch my fingers. I drop the lighter, curse through my teeth before I realize what I've done and apologize to God. Everything is harder than it should be these days.

Everything. Even talking to my mother. I have to avoid her, cutting our telephone conversations short. Or else she'd want to know the cause of this mixture of exhilaration and angst that clings to me like a thistle in wool, conjured by the fully packed suitcases under our bed. This thrill that translates into wide smiles, a spring in my step, a certain crazed light in my eye, which the Secret Service man doesn't know what to make of. Every Tuesday, the space between us seems to diminish, like two celestial orbs on tangential orbits, moving slowly toward collision. In the evening, I beg Liviu: We should jump into our car, drive away. "Soon, soon," he says. "Soon."

I find myself murmuring *soon, soon* at my father's grave. I tell him I am sorry, and I recite a prayer for his soul. I don't know many—just bits and pieces I've learned from Aunt Theresa. My mother has always been an overzealous communist, shunning all forms of religion.

"Not how we were raised," Aunt Theresa used to say.

"Hard to tell," I replied.

My mother doesn't talk about her childhood. She's ashamed that her parents had been wealthy landowners. My mother appears to be the most convinced communist you've ever known.

I don't know any more prayers, so I begin talking to my father. Aren't the dead the best listeners? Don't they have the sharpest ears? "Liviu and I are packing. We'll go. Don't be upset with me when I stop turning up at your grave, it's just that I went in search of a better life. You'd have been happy for me."

My father was incapable of being upset with me, but he thought his inability to punish and admonish made him a poor parent. He was in awe of my mother's strictness. And yet, when he drove me to school, he dropped me a few lei for an extra pretzel or a coveted cheese pie. One day, when my mother was away for a congress, he drove me to Bucharest, to the zoo. I ask him, "Do you remember? I never told anyone about that. Not my mother, anyway. I'm afraid of her. I tried to tell her,

God knows I did, but every time I open my mouth, I panic. She's so terrified of being left alone, that I don't know what she might do. You'll say, she always wants the best for me, but I begin to wonder. Help me, Dad. I don't know how much longer I can lie to her." I cross myself and realize that I began praying to him as if I was praying to one of the saints. Still, I go on. "Help me. Should I tell her or not? Could I live with myself if I go, never saying goodbye? After all she's done for me. Help me, Dad. Help me."

"I thought I might find you here."

My mouth snaps open and shut at the sound of my mother's voice. I turn. She stands as upright as the candle I just lit for my father, her patterned silk shirt flapping in the wind. She holds a bouquet of wildflowers.

"Mother," I say, and move to kiss her on the cheek. I wonder, *How much has she heard?* "Of course I'm here. It's the anniversary of Dad's death."

"And, obviously, I wasn't invited." She drops the wildflowers in front of my father's marble cross, then extracts cigarettes from her purse. She sits, legs crossed, on the neighboring grave, fenced by a mantel of polished white stone.

"Somebody is buried there," I say.

"And I think they wouldn't mind." She puffs her cheeks when she inhales. She only does this when she's angry. "You've been avoiding me."

"I've been busy," I say.

"Aren't we all? You look sick. Are you pregnant? I hope not."

She flicks her cigarette butt, and it lands on my father's grave. I pick it up, trying to avoid touching the traces of her lipstick. "Stop doing this. It's disrespectful."

She shrugs. "Habit."

Yes, the habit of disregarding my father, and his wishes. My cheeks are aflame. *What will I do if she asks?*

She gets up on her feet, straightening her skirt. "Let's have a cup of coffee. At your flat."

I think about the typewriter, about the empty space it left on our living room table after I'd sold it. "The pastry shop. Let me take you to a pastry shop. How would you like a creamy eclair? Or a chocolate amandine? My treat. For Dad."

She coils her arm around mine, and it feels like a python has attached itself to me, strangling.

"You're supposed to give handouts to people you don't know, in the name of the dead. Didn't Aunt Theresa tell you? I hear you're spending quite a lot of time together. I hear you also make day trips, to villages, for instance."

My knees melt, but she pulls me farther.

"You're hiding something from me, and, sooner or later, I will get to the bottom of this."

As we walk through the gate of the cemetery, I look toward the sink with cold water, where I always wash before leaving. It's custom—you wash your hands of sins, or you take them with you, to your home.

*In Which Alina Comes Home Early
from School on a Wednesday
Afternoon and Finds Her Mother at
Her House, Sitting in Front of the
Desk Where Alina Normally Grades
the Pupils' Papers, Going Through a
Bunch of Letters and a Notebook with
a Red Leather Cover*

"Mom! Is that my diary?"

The Curse

I'll be damned if I allow you to leave this country, to leave me all alone, to die alone, that's not what I raised you for. I could have had all the nice perfumes I wanted and dinners in town with your father, instead of scrubbing the poo off your clothes, getting the smell of burned oil out of my hair, but I did it all for you, and now you want to leave me, leave me? Never, never, never. I have *something*. What I have here, if you ever try to escape, if I ever hear anything, I'll call them. Border Security and the Secret Services will hear from me. I don't care if they bring you here in chains like a wild beast. A wild child you were, an ungrateful woman you've grown up to be, ungrateful to me, shame, shame, shame! Cursed, cursed, cursed you are, for being selfish and never thinking of me!

A Key on a Rope, a Shop, and a Beggar

Alina's childhood is a metal key dangling on a thick rope. It becomes warm under her uniform shirt (knee-long with white-and-blue squares), the blue apron (porous and stiff like the scrubber side of a dish sponge), the clip-on red pioneer tie. Her mother works as a seamstress and never picks her up from school—Alina always opens for herself the pressed cardboard door of her empty home. Sometimes a plate of cold food, prepared the evening before, awaits her. Sometimes there is nothing on the table.

Alina's childhood is a green backpack with two turtles in bright yellow and green, like the envy of her classmates. By the time she reaches fourth grade, the turtles are fissured and chipped, like Renaissance paintings. No amount of washing can remove the oily stains or the ballpoint-pen traces. She would like to hide the backpack, but there isn't enough room under her tight coat. It's also impossibly heavy as she walks to school. Her father only drives her in winter, when she arrives too early and has to wait for twenty minutes in the school playground. The teachers unlock the door at ten to eight. Until then, the children huddle, a colony of miserable penguins, while the wind mercilessly tugs at every patch of skin it catches uncovered, slips under sleeves and loose jackets to take a better bite. The gym teacher once unlocked the front door early and a foul mood drifted from their third-grade teacher that morning, instead of the smell of warm coffee and fresh lipstick.

Alina's childhood is lagging behind her two friends on her way home, stopping to stare at the windows of the foreign currency shop. Inside, there are wonders reserved for Westerners and leaders of the Party. The window is ten feet wide and as tall as a grown man. A heavy, green velvet curtain hides the riches inside from the sight of the passersby, but Alina has discovered that if she peers from a certain angle, she can see a corner of the refrigerator with its transparent doors. In it, slim, shapely bottles of Pepsi and Fanta are enclosed. She can also see an edge of the shelf housing the chocolates. Alina often dreams of them. Once, a couple, whom Alina will later think of as Germans, gave her a Toblerone as they came out of the shop. Alina has been writing to Santa for four Christmases, asking for it again. She dreams of the sticky chunks of clotted honey lingering on her tongue once the chocolate had melted.

The last day she stared through this window was during the summer vacation. Alina's skin was dark brown, her palms and knees were covered in crusts the color of rotten cherries. A woman with blond, permed hair and orange lipstick stepped out, clutching a plastic bag to her chest: a wonder unheard of. Alina prayed for the bag to break, to spill, to tear, so she could glimpse the marvels beneath the wrapping.

The woman leered at Alina for an instant, before she lifted her purse and struck her in the head. "Go beg somewhere else, little girl."

Alina yelped. The gaudy lipstick should have told her that the lady was neither a lady, nor a foreigner. It should have told her to step aside, and out of the woman's way.

The woman turned to the cavelike bowels of the shop and called, "Viorica, call the Police! There's a beggar outside—and we wouldn't want the tourists to see her!"

The side of her face ablaze from the blow and shame, Alina galloped home.

Now, when Alina is twenty-nine years old, the decadent West is a scintillating display window again that she isn't allowed to glimpse.

A Suitcase Full of Dreams

After her mother leaves, Alina paces the flat, clutching her diary: hallway to living room, to bedroom, to the kitchen, and back. The house tightens, and the walls move to squeeze the breath out of her. Alina goes to the bathroom, turns the water on, and places her head in the sink. The cold stream makes her scalp tingle. She listens to the liquid pouring down the drain, like her and Liviu's dreams.

Alina seeks the package of cigarettes she usually keeps for the Secret Service agent and sits in the kitchen. Water drips on her back, on the floor, while she chain-smokes. Her fingers tremble: anger or fear, she doesn't know. Her heart pounds her chest like a man trying to flee a building on fire. But they are both stuck.

When nausea claws at her stomach, Alina extinguishes her ninth cigarette. She darts to the bathroom. She throws up, and then remains on her knees, grasping the toilet seat. How will she ever tell Liviu that it's over? That there was no point to all the preparations they've made: the car, the tent, the foreign currency they've exchanged. The two suitcases under their bed, packed with their best clothes. Alina can't sit around any longer, she must unpack.

The suitcase is made of reddish-brown leather. Alina opens it and begins peeling out its contents. Her angora sweater. A winter coat made of rabbit skin Liviu bought for her birthday just before Mihai defected. The silver brooch shaped like a daisy, the one her father gave her the year she went to college. It's time to put the precious trinkets back where they belong. It's time to deplete the suitcase full of dreams.

Alina opens the door of her bedroom wardrobe. She caresses the lacquered oak. It gleamed golden when they bought it, the year when Liviu and she married. Its surface was smooth like a baby's skin. Now, it's full of long cracks, and inflorescences, like the ones that remain on a windscreen when it hails. Its bruised surface reminds Alina of her own marriage. What will Liviu say when he comes home?

She begins extracting her belongings from the gaping mouth of her suitcase, places them on the shelves. They're full of cardigans she never really liked: the knitted sort, with colorful geometric patterns. The ones she could find in the Universal store, grayish and always half empty. Her pearl-colored angora sweater looks dejected—like a Russian princess when the communists came to power. So does her fine crepe dress the color of sand, surrounded by brown skirts and a dirty-blue two-piece. Her mother can find fine fabrics, and sew so well, but she never makes the time, not for her. Her own mother. Her mother.

Alina opens Liviu's suitcase. She arranges the delicate flax shirts among the other slightly discolored ones, with starched collars that scratch his neck raw. Alina pauses. She remembers a wooden chest at the foot of her grandparents' bed, containing all their clothes, and their linen sheets. Why should she and Liviu need more in order to be happy?

And then, she knows: Their closet should be purged. They should have their fresh start, even here, in Romania. Alina is determined. What would they have wanted in Germany or France, anyway?

Alina drags the garbage bin into the room, like a wounded prisoner. She tosses in Liviu's old shirts, her fluffy pullovers. But soon, there isn't enough room. Alina stamps the clothes with her foot, flattening them. She twists and pushes, grinding her teeth. She jumps on one foot. It's like pressing grapes into juice, but without the grapes, without the joy, the atmosphere of celebration. It's the opposite of merrymaking. She wishes the clothes compressed to the point of disappearance, out of her home, out of her life. She wants to crush them. But they bob their ugly folds up and out of the bin as soon as she lifts her leg. She needs reinforcements, and perhaps some new containers. Alina ransacks the kitchen drawers. Wrenches, screwdrivers, knives, sponges, even one plastic tablecloth, fly onto the brown tiles on the floor, defeated bodies on a bloodied battle-field.

In the bedroom, she brutalizes the clothes into the canvas bags she brought from the kitchen. Filled carriers suffocate the corridor between the bed and the wall, as she rearranges the fine garments destined for their journey in the empty closet. Alina steps back. The trembling has subsided. She must carry on in the living room.

Alina doesn't have any more canvas bags, so she uses cotton sheets to hoard the trinkets displayed in her glass cabinet: a sitting man who holds a fishing net, a group of flamingos, a ballet dancer, sets of cups and plates. When she's done, there are only six whiskey glasses left on display, made of Bohemian crystal.

Alina is out of breath and out of sheets, but she wants to continue the purge. She remembers there are burlap sacks in the cellar. She darts downstairs, loots the basement. One of the sacks still holds potatoes—she spills them onto the floor.

Back on the landing, she stops, transfixed. The door is wide open. Has she lost her mind? Or has someone broken in? She steps slowly, trying to steady her breath. Liviu stands in the hallway, turning his head in all directions.

"Alina, what have you done?"

His words are like a slap. Alina finally looks around. She sees the empty furniture, their belongings scattered on the floor, or packed in bags. As if an evil spirit had turned their house upside down and shook out its contents. As if it were the house of someone who was on the brink of moving out.

Except they never will.

They never will, and she must tell Liviu.

Alina begins trembling. She doesn't know if it's anger, or fear, or if she's disintegrating.

The Trip

On Tuesday, Alina waits for the Secret Service man with vanilla-and-lemon-cream homemade cakes. Just before he arrives, she manages to change into a pair of long, shapeless trousers and a turtleneck sweater, even though it's early June. Alina will bake under wool by the time he's done with the questioning—but these are the least provocative clothes she has.

The Secret Service man arrives half an hour before scheduled. He grabs her hand when she opens the door and pulls her down her stairs.

"We're going on a trip today," he says.

Alina pulls back. "Let me just take my purse."

She steps inside, pausing on the threshold. Her heart knocks on her ribs, trying to break them. She wonders, how easy would it be to turn and lock the door? What would *he* do then?

Instead, Alina drapes the chain of her purse around her shoulder and follows him down the stairs. In front of her apartment building, a van is parked on the curb. It's green, and its windows are obscured. Alina steps back, but the Secret Service man grabs her elbow and pulls her gently. With his other hand, he unlocks the back door. He pushes her inside. Alina allows herself to be herded. Her mind is a blank sheet. When he blindfolds her, she manages to wail a "Where are you taking me? What have I done?" among short rasps of breath.

"Shh," he says. "I'm not hurting you. Not today."

She feels his fingertips brushing her face, her hands. She hears a metal clanking, and cold bracelets closing around her wrists.

"For your own safety," he says.

Alina sobs. "Please, I haven't done anything," she says. "It was all pretend, I was just—"

The door slams.

As the car rocks and sways, Alina wonders what her mother has done. What she has told the agent. If she will be beaten, tortured, mutilated for it. Why? Why? Why? Alina barely represses an urge to pee. She can hardly breathe. Why would her own mother do this?

After an eternity, the car stops. The Secret Service man helps her climb down from the van, but leaves her blindfold tied. Alina is trembling, and she can't see, so she leans on the man next to her. His fingertips linger on the back of her hand. Alina wants to pull away, to scream and run. Instead, she allows him to touch her.

They step into a building. Alina can feel the air changing, the lack of sunlight on her skin. A smell of rotten food, sweat, and mold. Her mind races, trying to invent a convincing lie to tell the man once he begins to question her about the diary. There are voices around her. She can't distinguish the words, but there are barked orders, screams, and yelps of pain. Alina pulls closer to the Secret Service man. He wraps a hand around her back, moving downward, massaging her behind. Alina wants to tell him to stop. She doesn't.

They descend stairs, many of them, until Alina begins feeling dizzy. The man greets various other persons, who answer back. The silence between salutations is marked by shrill wails, like the ones of dying animals. This is either a torture center or an abattoir.

They stop, and the Secret Service man undoes her blindfold.

"Look!" he says, pointing below.

They stand on a metal platform, raised around an enclosed yard. In it, two guards, ordering about a dozen prisoners. They're dirty, they have long, filthy beards, and their clothes are in rags. They're so thin that their cheekbones, their elbows look like they might pierce through their skin anytime.

"Look," says the Secret Service man, "these are dissidents. Conspirators against the state, enemies of the people. And that one is a priest."

Alina glances where the Secret Service man is pointing, but her vision is blurred. She's sick. She pants, trying not to throw up. He grabs her hand, pushes her down a flight of stairs. They descend for a long time, past lighted windows, and into what seems to be a cellar. The screams grow louder. Alina stops.

"Come, come, don't be afraid," he says.

She curses her mother in her mind. Curses her to die slowly, in the most horribly imaginable pains, and burn in hell for all eternity. She'll try to tell the Secret Service man that it wasn't her diary where she wrote about their plans to defect. That it was a work of fiction. That she hasn't come to the ending yet, where the Agents of the Motherland discover the defectors, and punish them for their treason. She'll tell him, *my mother has gotten it all wrong.*

The screams are unbearable, nails drilled in Alina's eardrums, when they stop in front of a great iron door. The Secret Service man pushes it open. In front of them gapes a long corridor with doors on each side. On each door, there's a metal panel.

The Secret Service man holds her hand, walks to the middle of the corridor, then stops. He slides open one of the panels, pushing Alina forward. Inside, a naked man is tied to a chair, black and blue with bruises and congealed blood. A guard is hitting him with a shovel. The prisoner barely rouses, his head moving from one side to the other when the blows fall. Alina screams.

"A defector," says the Secret Service man, sliding the panel shut.

Punish. Punish. Curse.

The Secret Service agent places his hand over Alina's mouth. She's still screaming.

"Shut up," he says.

He's smiling. He wraps his hand around Alina's waist.

"Come, let's have some privacy, huh?"

He pulls her toward him, and she falls on all fours. Her knees have turned to mush. Alina doesn't belong to herself anymore, she's his, he can do as he pleases, she must trust him, can she trust him? What will he do to her?

He forces her up, throws her on his back like a sack of potatoes. Alina cries, biting her fists, drawing blood.

The Secret Service man stops in front of the last door on the corridor and swings it open. A chamber illuminated by a weak light bulb. A concrete floor, dusty and smudged. She'd rather not think what caused the stains. A table and two chairs. The man eases her onto one of the seats. He caresses her hand.

"Have I upset you?"

Tears flow down Alina's cheeks. She tries to speak, but her tongue is made of lead.

The Secret Service man kisses her hand, then moves to the chair opposite her. From his breast pocket, he pulls a notebook the size of his hand, and a pencil.

"Comrade Mungiu, on October 15th last year, pupil Atanasiu brought contraband items to school. I was given to understand that you facilitated the escape of the said pupil. Is that true?"

"N-no. No."

Alina repeats in her mind the words of her statement, like the poems her children learn by heart: *It was a novel I was trying to write. In the end, the Agents of the Revered Motherland catch the wrongdoers, punish them. It was destined to be informative for the children. Curse my mother.*

"Comrade, has your brother-in-law, the traitor of kin and country, Mihai Mungiu, ever contacted you?"

Alina tries to steady her breath. "No. No. Never."

I was trying to write a novel. The ending where the Agents of the Revered Motherland catch the wrongdoers, punish them. Informative for the children. Curse my mother.

The Secret Service man scribbles in his notebook. "Comrade, have you noticed any suspicious activity taking place in your school? Abnormal behavior in your pupils?"

"No, never." He's trying to lull her into a fake feeling of security. She must remain alert. "I would have reported it immediately to you, or to our head-mistress. It's my duty as a citizen, as a teacher."

Trying to write a novel. The ending: Agents of the Revered Motherland catch the wrongdoers. Punish them. Informative for the children. Curse my mother.

"Comrade Mungiu." The Secret Service agent folds his notebook shut, looks into her eyes. The scar above his eye is purplish-red. "Have you noticed any suspicious activity in your husband? Signs that he might be attempting to leave our Motherland?"

Around them, the screams rise again, a dissonant symphony of suffering. It would be easy to turn her husband in. To say that he's the one trying to defect. She'd never have problems with the Secret Services again. Alina breathes in sharply. This, or being raped and beaten to death. And only God knows what in between.

"Comrade Mungiu?"

Alina places her hands on the table, her palms upward. They are trembling. "No. Never. If I had, I would have reported it to you. It's my duty as a citizen. For the Motherland."

The Secret Service agent nods. "Even your husband?"

Novel. Ending. Agents of the Revered Mother-land. Punish. Punish. Curse.

"Even my husband."

He jumps up. His chair screeches on the concrete. He steps toward her, the handcuffs in his hands. "We're done here."

"Where are we going?" she whimpers.

"You'll see."

He blindfolds her again.

"Where are you taking me? Why? We haven't done anything. Please—"

"Shut up. And move."

They pass by the torture chambers: Alina can tell by the screaming. She moves quickly, quicker than him. *Please don't stop. Not here.*

Alina is relieved when they begin climbing stairs. She rushes, misses a rung. She tumbles down, the sharp edges of the steps like so many knives in her ribs. He catches her hand, pulls her up.

"Why the hurry?" His tone is gleeful.

Alina wants to claw his eyes out, give him a reason never to smile again.

Soon, they're outside. The air grows lighter, warmer. She hears a car door opening, and he shoves her into the van.

The tin has become hot in the sunlight, and Alina feels like she's in an oven. She thinks of the iron bull; the gruesomest torture instrument she knows. A fire lit below the bull's belly, where an unfortunate soul roasted: a slow, slow, slow, unimaginably painful death.

Alina is wondering what they will do to her, when the van jolts to a halt. She can hear her own teeth clattering in her mouth, as someone fumbles with the door.

"Easy, there's a step," says the Secret Service agent.

He uncuffs her, undoes her blindfold, then steps back behind the steering wheel, without a word. Alina wants to call him. Where is he leaving her? She crumples on the sidewalk. She needs minutes to realize she's in front of her apartment building, and that she peed herself.

*

When Liviu arrives, and crawls into their bed, Alina has long cried herself to sleep. She stirs. His smell of cheap tobacco and stale alcohol make her open her eyes. They're sore and swollen.

"What's the matter?" says Liviu, seeking her mouth.

She pushes him aside, turns her back toward him, facing the wall. She tells him about her day.

When she's done, Liviu's speech is no longer slurred. "Alina, sweetheart. I'm so sorry. I don't know what to say." Liviu sits up. "There's nothing I can say. Nothing I can do." He punches the wall behind him. "Nothing." He caresses her back, and this time, Alina doesn't pull away. "Only magic, only a wonder could save us."

What Even Aunt Theresa
Fears

Aunt Theresa is the most fearless creature Alina has ever known. She asks Alina, *Who did you vote for?* on Election Day, even though there is a single option on the ballot. She asks in a loud voice, while the windows are wide open. But Alina would be fearless, too, if she had a son in the Secret Services and another one working for Border Security, like her aunt.

Aunt Theresa gives Alina foreign currency she makes her sons buy through less-than-official channels. She also asks, *How are your preparations going? When will you be leaving?* Usually, Alina says, *Good. We are making lists of what we need. Soon.* But not today.

Today Alina says, *We are not leaving. We will stay.* Her voice has the cadence of a marching legion. *I'll watch them tear my husband apart, one small piece after the other, until there are only shadows.*

Aunt Theresa says, *Why? Why?*

My mother has something, Alina says. *I don't know what it is. I caught her going through my things last week, when I came home from work.*

Alina is trembling. *Today, I made her return my spare key. She said she knows what I want to do. She said that I shouldn't even try to reach the border, that she'll make sure that I'd come back in handcuffs. I don't know what she has. I don't know what she'll do. She hates Liviu. She hates him. And the Secret Service agent—*

Alina's voice breaks off. She can't even speak about the horrors she saw. She can't even think that, one of these days, she might be one of those prisoners. She or Liviu.

Aunt Theresa says nothing. She closes the windows and turns on the water in the kitchen. The stream makes Alina think of all the tears she is bound to cry. But Aunt Theresa kneels in front of her, pulls her ear toward her lips.

There is something we can do, she says.

Alina's fingers claw around her own skirt, squeezing. Implausible, but there is something that even Aunt Theresa fears and makes her speak in subdued tones.

You need to find Saint Friday. There is no other way. You must go into the woods on the shortest night of the year—

Long Forgotten

There are a dozen of them in the clearing, ghostly silhouettes in their white skirts and shirts, with their embroidered vests and necklaces made of golden coins, or at least so it seems from the bush where Alina is hiding. They could be peasant girls, for all she knows, though their chant is in a language Alina has never heard before, many *z*'s and *j*'s and *dz*'s filling the air like a swarm of angry bees. This is a language long forgotten. Forgotten are their dances, the hops, the swings in their hips, the circles they draw with their toes, their twirls and whirls. They gather in a circle and begin spinning, faster, faster, faster, until their very contours fade and the clearing seems an impressionistic picture of itself with the ghostly essence of the *Sânziene** slipping from them and imbibing the woods, the grass, the creek. In the shortest night of the year, the fairies walk, or rather, dance the Earth. Alina must wait for her chance, and her odds are good. Her

* *Romanian name for fairies and name of the annual festival that celebrates them.*

heart is thumping at her ribs, attempting to break them. She jolts, rustling the leaves with every crack she hears. She hopes her moment will come soon.

They do not tire of spinning, or so it seems, while Alina's eyes feel increasingly swollen and every whisper of the wind makes her want to run home. But now it's too late, because it's happening. No men have come, so they must scour the woods for them. The first one who broke loose from the dancing mass went in the opposite direction, but the second is coming toward her. Alina's hands clutch the cable wire, slippery with her sweat. One step at a time, barely touching the rug of decomposing leaves, the *Sânziana* comes singing toward her. Alina first catches her scent, of flowers, hay, and overripe fruit. The heat of the fairy's body makes her feel faint, but she grinds her teeth, and when a skinny shin is in sight, she tackles the *Sânziana* to the ground, stuffing a folded handkerchief in her mouth. She turns the gagging fairy on her belly and holds her down, while tying her hands with the cable cord. It's not very hard, because the fairy is slim and her bones are brittle like a pigeon's. When Alina is done, she pulls the *Sânziana* to her feet and drags her by the cord toward the barren hill. The fairy fights and bends and shakes in seizures, howling through the handkerchief. Alina grabs her by the hair and tugs harder until she feels it ripping in her hands. The fairy follows, and where tears fall from her eyes the grass becomes yellow and parched.

When they arrive at the top of the hill, they are both

out of breath. The *Sânziana* yanks herself upward and tries to run, but Alina pulls her back. The cord cuts through the flesh in her palm, and it burns deeper and deeper as the fairy twitches and jerks. She suddenly turns and rams her like a bull, knocking Alina off her feet. They both fall to the ground, and the fairy bangs her head against Alina's teeth. Alina slaps her, rolls on top of her, and begins hitting the *Sânziana* with her fists. Her screams are muffled by the handkerchief in her mouth, and as she gulps for air, she gags. She brings her tiny hands to her swelling face, but they cannot protect her, and Alina is coming in swinging, right, and left, and right, and after each blow she hears bones grinding and she doesn't know if they're hers or the fairy's, when something blunt kicks her in the shoulder, throwing her off balance and onto her back.

Her mouth is full of salty blood, and there is a dull ache in her front teeth and in her knuckles and a not-so-dull-pain in her shoulder. She looks up and she sees an old lady with wrinkles as deep as cuts, smiling at her, revealing a lone front tooth. A few white, wispy hairs are falling to her shoulders. She scrambles into a sitting position. The old lady is wearing a thick, worn wool coat in the middle of the summer, and her back is bent at almost ninety degrees. She supports herself on a gnarled cane, which Alina identifies as the object that knocked her off balance. Tears begin to flow from Alina's eyes, slim riverbeds on her face covered in yellow, powdery dust.

"Saint Friday . . . Please . . . Help me!"

The Potion

Saint Friday said, *Take this. Put a few drops of the potion into her tea.*

I said, *She doesn't drink tea. Does coffee work?*

Saint Friday said, *Yes, it does. Seven drops for a cup.*

How was I ever to make my mother coffee if we haven't spoken for months? I wondered for a long time. I knew all the right answers, but I blindfolded myself and went through my days stumbling with every step. Stumbling until my soul ached with the bruises. But when Liviu fell asleep on the living room floor, drunk and crying, on a Wednesday evening, I knew that it was time. On the Monday that followed it, I stayed in bed and called in sick at school. Then the waiting began. I suspected my mother had a copy of the spare key she'd given me back—and I hoped to be wrong.

I said, *What does it do?*

Saint Friday said, *Do you know "The Story of the Pig"?*

"The Story of the Pig" is one of my favorite stories. A prince is turned into a pig by an evil witch, but his princess wife saves him by retrieving three magical objects.

I always wanted to be that princess. Save someone. But I can't even save myself. I have no saving to spare for anyone else.

I said, *I hope I'm not turning my mother into a pig.*

She said, *No, but it's the same principle. Even better. After she drinks it, you'll be able to immerse her into water or other liquids for an uncertain amount of time.*

I said, *How long is that? And why would I want to do that?*

She said, *Hours at least, maybe days. Nobody knows precisely. And you'll want to remember this.*

I waited. I passed my time on the couch, a book in my hands, pretending to read while my thoughts revolved around their own axis like a drunken, hurried planet. On Thursday, I shuddered when I heard the key turn in the lock. The front door opened, and there she stood, with her formidable mink coat and rabbit-fur hat.

I told my mother, *Hello. Would you like a cup of coffee?* and hurried to the kitchen even before she had taken her gloves off. My heart was beating like a rabbit chased by a legion of greyhounds. When the water began boiling in the kettle, so did my blood. I'd been right. She'd made a copy of her spare key, the one I'd asked her to return to me. I counted to steady my hands: two spoonfuls of coffee for each cup. Boil the mixture three times. Three minutes for the coffee dust to settle. After pouring, seven drops of potion for a cup.

I said, *You're a saint. How come you're allowed to do this?*

Saint Friday said, *I'm not allowed to give you something that would kill her. I would then be breaking the sixth commandment.*

I said, *But I'm breaking the fifth.*

She said, *Not quite. I am assuming that you're doing this in your mother's best interest.*

I said, *I am.*

Saint Friday said, *There you go.*

*

My mother asked me, *What are you doing at home? Shouldn't you be in school? Did you put sugar in my coffee?*

I asked her, *What are you doing in my house when I should be in school? How did you open my door?*

She said, *You know I like my coffee black.*

I said, *Don't drink it, then,* almost hoping that she wouldn't.

She drank it like a glass of vodka, bottoms up, contorting her face after she was done.

She said, *I take whatever crumbs my daughter throws me. Now, could I please have a coffee? Black?*

In the kitchen, I sank into a chair and waited, trembling.

She screamed, *Alina! Alina!*

When I returned to the living room, she was shrinking by the moment. Before I reached the armchair where she was sitting, she was the size of a baby. I frantically peeled the clothes off her, for fear that they might suffocate her. When I was done, she was two middle fingers tall. Perhaps a bit plumper. Naked, cold, scared, wrinkled, and small.

I cut a patch from her skirt, to wrap her up in something until I stripped a doll for some clothing. She kept striking me with her little fists, asking, *Why have you done this to me? Why, Alina, why?* I tried to carry her with me around the house, as I paced, thinking, crying, mumbling, *I'm sorry, I'm sorry, I'm sorry.* When she bit me, I put her in the empty fishbowl for her own safety. But she stripped herself and began pounding her fists against the glass, screaming, *Have you done this because I won the lottery?* I said, *Please, Mom, you won the equivalent of two years of your pension,* and I poured warm water on top of her, filling half of the bowl, drowning all of her sounds, and then I put it on top of a radiator, so that she wouldn't get cold.

*

I said, *I don't know if I want to do this anymore.*
 Saint Friday said, *I also think you shouldn't.*
 I said, *But I need to escape.*
 Saint Friday said, *You're running in the wrong direction.*
 I said, *How do I know which the right direction is?*
 Saint Friday said, *First, you stop.*

Now, Everything Has Changed

6:17 a.m.

Alina wakes up to an empty bed, even before her alarm clock rings. Liviu must have left an hour ago—or else he wouldn't have caught the train that takes him to school on time. Before she goes to the bathroom to wash her face, she checks on her mother. She's still resting in her transparent bowl, wrapped in a piece of soft fabric cut from a fluffy yellow duvet.

There's cold coffee on the kitchen table, made by Liviu earlier. Alina pours herself a cup, and a few drops in a thimble for her mother. She also brings her apricot pie crumbs. Her mother is awake, and watches her through narrowed eye slits. It's been more than two weeks since the shrinking, two in which Alina has done little else but cry. Her mother threatened, cursed, and swore. All in a shrill, thin voice. But as anything else in life, even guilt eventually wears off. Now her mother refuses to speak.

7:25 a.m.

Alina drinks another cup of coffee in the teachers' break room. She's clutching the purse in her lap. Her mother, in a pink perfume bottle, has begun with the rocking and the banging for the day. Alina shakes her knees to hide the movements in her purse. Everyone stares at her, in silence. Even Miss Puiu forgets what she was saying about her seven siblings and her mother's polenta.

Before class, her pupils sing "The Tricolor Flag." Alina moves her lips, but she refuses to sing along. She has no love for her country, for the government, for the Beloved Leader. She can't believe in a regime that encourages brother turning on brother, mothers on their children. A regime that punishes innocent people.

8:26 a.m.

Romanian Literature class. Today's story is about the *voievod* Ştefan the Great and his mother. Most of Alina's pupils stare at their textbooks. A few of them glare at her lecturing desk. The rocking in her purse makes the soft brown leather wobble. Alina smiles and hides it under her chair, which rests on a wooden dais. The pedestal she sits on makes her feel uncomfortable today.

9:10 a.m.

Mathematics. Her mother taps through her leather wrapping on the wooden dais. Alina wants to dig her heel into the purse and crush, crush, crush until she hears the crunch of glass and tiny bones and blood. She'd throw her purse in the first garbage bin, without even looking inside.

But she doesn't. Instead, she smiles and assures the children that the noise is caused by wood-boring beetles.

During the ten-minute break between classes, she locks herself in a toilet and promises her mother that this is the last time she's taking her to school. Her mother pouts and crosses her arms. Alina hisses, "No food for you today, missy!"

1:40 p.m.
Alina prepares fried chicken thighs with mashed potatoes. She places her mother's bottle on the table, so she can watch her eat. Her mother says, "I hope a bone catches in your throat."

Alina cackles.

3:45 p.m.
It's Tuesday, and the Secret Service agent is due to arrive soon. Alina checks the bedroom, to make sure no corner of the suitcases peek from under the bed. She places her mother between the sweaters she's packed for their escape. She arranges a plate of the apricot cakes on the living room table, makes fresh coffee.

4:20 p.m.
The Secret Service agent hasn't arrived yet. Alina runs from window to window, listens to the sounds

on the staircase. Nothing. She pulls from the drawer of her cupboard an unsigned postcard she'd received the day before. "THINKING OF YOU," it says on the back, in capital letters. On the front, there's a picture of the sea promenade at Constanţa, the one Alina has known since she was a student and played tour guide for German tourists. Liviu declared his love on that promenade.

5:10 p.m.

Alina concludes that the Secret Service man must be on vacation, and that the postcard was from him. She begins preparing dinner. Today, she makes potato stew with smoked ham.

8:23 p.m.

After Alina and Liviu have eaten, they step into the living room. Alina turns the TV and the radio up loud and whispers in Liviu's ear. "How much longer? Are you sure we should wait for the Italian visa? Wouldn't it be safer to leave now?"

As she tells him about her day, and how unmanageable her mother has become, Alina remembers with a shudder that she left her parent in the suitcase. She darts toward the bedroom and tosses the suitcase open. She can't find the bottle; she can't find it. She ejects all her clothes on the floor, while crying and screaming, "It's gone, it's gone!"

Alina is sorry, she's so sorry for what she's done, and for what she's doing to her mother, who never deserved this, not even for all the harm she's done to her.

Liviu steps into the room. "What's gone?"

"My mother!"

Liviu bends, fumbling with the sweaters. Alina searches the hidden pockets inside the suitcase. She hears the sound of a glass rolling on the floor. Alina turns so sharply that pain pierces her neck muscles like an arrow. Liviu holds the pink metal bottle with the tips of his fingers. He can't even look at her.

"She's here, she's here."

Guilt tugs hard at Alina's frayed edges.

Ripping

Aunt Theresa has given us a can of gasoline so we can go for a drive with our new used car.

The upholstery inside has oil stains and cigarette holes as wide as my pinky. It smells like a woman who has spent her whole afternoon in a bar, chain-smoking and drinking cheap vodka while being felt up by the man beside her, who's drunker than she is.

My husband and I are going out for a picnic. My favorite spot is in the woods near the monastery, a place I've known since I was a little girl. But we have to leave the tarmac and drive on a path of dry earth for the last section of the road. This rusting heap of metal we call a car squeaks and moans while the dust rises around us like we're in a sandstorm.

"Is this normal?" I ask.

"Yes," says Liviu. "The car's just fine."

"I can't believe that we paid more for this piece of crap than for a new one."

"What were you going to do?"

Nothing. The average Romanian waits for a new car for up to eight years. But after the defection of my brother-in-law, we have been demoted from the rank of "comrade" to that of "persona non grata." We would never have stood a chance to get our hands on a new Dacia.

"I'm sorry you had to sell your stamps," I say.

"I'm sorrier for your earrings."

"Don't worry about it. Aunt Theresa will give them back to me. Somehow."

No matter how green the foliage is, on the ground of the forest are always dead leaves, a permanent reminder of the autumn. I spread our blanket on top of them, near the dirty creek I fell in at least a dozen times when I was little. My mother always brought a spare set of clothing for me.

"Shit!"

"What is it?" Liviu asks.

"I left my mother at home."

Liviu rolls his eyes.

"Great!"

"We're fine. We don't have to go. I pulled her out of the bowl and placed her in the perfume bottle. I just forgot her on the kitchen counter."

"Fabulous. The kitchen counter."

"Don't worry. I put her in the metal container I use every time we take her out. Even if the Secret Services spontaneously decide to search our house, they won't find her. You can't see through the bottle; and what would they want with a bottle of perfume?"

He starts folding the blanket.

"Alina, really, when will you start behaving like

a grown-up? You always manage to pull something like this."

"You know what? I never should have told you."

I'm schlepping the heavy straw basket from the trunk, hoping that Liviu will change his mind.

"You honestly think that I wouldn't notice? And besides, we're talking about your mother here, Alina, for God's sake!"

Yes. My mother. My mother who dug out our dirty little secret by going through my things while I was not at home. My mother who was blackmailing us into staying put and swallowing all the crap the government made us eat. My mother who had it coming.

So yes, when Liviu invokes God and my mother in the same sentence, I shrug. Liviu drags the picnic basket back into the car.

"You know, I'd like to do something that doesn't involve my mother for one time this month," I say.

Liviu shakes his head.

"Did you leave her there on purpose? After what you've done to her?"

On the little mound on the other bank of the creek, three poppies have sprouted from the compost. I'd like to crush their petals between my lips.

"Do you really think she would have enjoyed the picnic? Should we have set her free so she could scurry off? Only to be eaten tonight by a fox?" I muse.

"You're unbelievable. Let's go."

I sit on the bed of leaves. The earth is cool, but my blood is boiling.

"Alina! Let's go. The poor woman—"

"Yes. The poor woman. That's not what you called her until I took care of the problem. *I* took care of the problem, because you were busy calling her names. Busy not staining your white hands. Your failed-archaeologist hands."

"Alina, this is not the time—"

Liviu steps into the car and starts the engine. He knows that I won't let him wait forever. We only have a canister of gasoline, and if we run out of fuel, we have to get home on foot.

I get up and before I get into the car, I jump over to the other bank and pick a poppy, though I know that it will wilt in the car.

On our way back home, I insert my finger into one of the cigarette burns on the upholstery and tug lightly, so that my husband won't hear the fabric ripping.

What Alina Did Last Tuesday

It's Tuesday, and when she comes home from work, Alina runs up the stairs of her apartment building and stumbles into the kitchen. Her mother knocked over her fishbowl yesterday and unhooked the telephone, so Alina and Liviu spent the whole evening scouring the apartment for her, until they looked inside the shoe closet. She was inside a pair of ancient boots Alina uses when they go fishing, and the smell of dirty socks was caught in her hair. Alina had to pour water over her again when she left for work, to prevent her from making too much noise, and placed the bowl in the kitchen sink, where it could not be tilted.

Alina exhales—her mother is where she left her. She bends, dipping two fingers into the water, when she hears the doorbell.

She opens the door and there is the Secret Service man, three hours early, looming on the threshold like a bad omen.

"Comrade Mungiu," he says, stepping in, without taking off his hat. "Please join me at headquarters."

"Excuse me?"

Alina takes two steps back, swinging the door, but the man catches her wrist.

"Comrade Mungiu, are you resisting?"

"No!" she cries.

The man pulls again. Alina sways by him, pushing the door shut. She stands between him and the exit.

"Comrade, this is ridiculous!" he says, tightening his grip.

Alina lowers her hand, relaxing her muscles, then abruptly pushes him aside and makes to run. He catches her skirt from behind, pulling her closer. He throws a hand across her chest, pressing her against him. Alina kicks and screams.

"Comrade!"

Alina can feel that he is hard. There is a knot tightening in her throat, but there is only one thing she can do. Her body grows limp, and she leans backward closing her eyes, rubbing her buttocks against his member through the thin skirt.

"Are you sure that I can't give you what you need here, in my home?"

*

Alina steps into the kitchen and throws the plastic tablecloth over the bowl. She fills a pot with water and places it on the stove. Her own guilt for shrinking her mother forgotten, she considers putting the bowl containing her mother on the other stove burner, but she has no time for shenanigans. The man must have his coffee.

He took his pants off in the living room and leaned against the back of the couch.

"I like it very much when women kiss me down there," he said, pointing toward his dangling, swelling penis. It was short and thick, a sausage made by a clumsy housewife.

A sausage. Alina tried to keep thinking about a sausage, with her eyes shut.

"You haven't done this very often, have you?" he finally asked.

Alina swallowed a tear and tried to smile, but out came a frightened giggle.

"I'll tell you what to do, no problem. See, you should grab it like this, rub, and put it in your mouth," he said.

In the kitchen, Alina wipes her mouth furiously. She would love to fill it with dish detergent and scour it, but the man might taste it on her.

"I have some sour-cherry cake from yesterday. Would you like some?" she asks.

"Yes, thank you," he says.

As she opens the cupboard, looking for powdered sugar, Alina sees the vinegar and grabs it. On a whim, she uncovers the bowl and drizzles the vinegar over her mother. Her mother's eyes grow wide before she closes them tightly and starts rubbing.

*

The man gone, Alina grabs her mother by the back of her dress. Her mother spits and screams and tries to scratch her. Alina, eyes reddened like a mad dog's, dips her mother in the water in the toilet bowl.

"If you make one more move, I'm dropping you and flushing. Do you understand?"

Her mother thrashes once more. Alina dips her leg into the water. Alina's mother stops, frozen.

"Why?" she tweets.

"You heartless bitch. Do you know what the man from the Secret Services told me, after doing me from behind? Twice? That you contacted them yesterday with some information. Concerning me and Liviu. About a planned escape from the country."

Alina drops her mother lower and lower as she speaks. Now her mother chokes on the toilet water, coughing.

"You bitch. I'll make sure that you never, ever return to your original size. Do you hear me?"

Alina's mother shrieks, gulping for air.

Alina's face is as hard as the marble that statues are made of. "You. Fucking. Degenerate. Bitch."

The White Line

There's a white strip in the middle of the road, and our car is following it into the night. The weak headlights of this squeaky, rusting heap of metal only manage to light a few yards of line in front of us, but I know the road goes beyond that, and it will go on and on and on until it turns into metallic booths at the border, toward noon. It will be the perfect time to cross it—the Border Security agents will be tired, waiting for the shift to change, not so thorough, not so rough. After the booth, there will be another white line, and at its end we will finally meet our new selves. This line is life. My new life.

Since Tuesday, I've been wondering if the harm I've done is larger or smaller than the one that's been done to me. Guilt has been creeping slowly, but firmly. What happened Tuesday is my fault, too. I paid for a wrong I was committing—trying to creep out of this damned country. Evil deeds will always be punished. At least, that's what my mother told me.

Tuesday evening, when Liviu came home, he found me tossing heaps of clothes on top of the suitcases, their mouths like those of three hungry crocodiles.

We have to go, I told him, between sobs. *Now. Today. Tomorrow, at the latest.*

He asked what happened and held me tight, but I wrenched myself free and told him nothing. His embrace made me want to scream.

Later, when he opened the bathroom door, he saw me in the tub, staring at the dish-washing scrubber. I had been wondering for an hour: If I scoured the soiled patches of skin until they turned raw, would the blood wash me clean?

Bottled Goods

The light in the Border Security interrogation room
has a greenish hue, just like the bile coming up in her
mouth. Alina has to swallow it down over and over
again, leaving a burning highway in its wake. This
always happens when she doesn't eat in an entire day,
but that's just how long it takes for a team of men
to disassemble a Dacia, looking for hidden money
or jewelry. Something that could serve them should
they, God forbid, attempt to flee to the West. You
only forsake your country by going to Heaven, and
the communist government doesn't believe in that,
either. The Border Security agents don't believe that
she and Liviu are only going on vacation to Germany.
They also don't know that they won't find her greatest secret upon her. It lies where secrets belong in all
adventure stories—buried in the woods.

But it has been almost a day since they've been
held up at the border, and Alina imagines her mother's tiny fists banging against the glass wall that may
prove to be her coffin. She never thought it would be
so long before she could make the rescuing call.

Though it is something she shouldn't do, Alina buries her face in her palms and begins to pray.

On the night before they left, she and Liviu drove to their favorite picnic spot in the woods, near the monastery. They dug a hole with two tablespoons and their hands. That was where they lowered the perfume bottle containing her mother, careful not to wake her. She had fallen asleep in the car—Alina could see her through the transparent pinkish glass. Strangely, Alina remembered Snow White's story, though she knew there would be no prince to give her mother the kiss of life.

Alina laid her in the ground, not far from where she and Aunt Theresa had buried her grandfather, and made the sign of the cross three times, for good luck.

As they were driving toward the border, the silence between her and Liviu was thicker than the darkness. Through the window, Alina could only distinguish the shadowy contours of the trees on the side of the road and nothing beyond them.

"I don't understand why you couldn't just leave her with Theresa," said Liviu in the car, cutting through the silence.

"I told you. She wouldn't have taken her. I'll just call her when we reach Yugoslavia and tell her where to find Mother."

"Why when we cross the border? Why not call her when we leave—or when we're on our way?" asked Liviu, drumming his fingers on the wheel.

Alina shook her head. "No, no. She'd never touch my mother. She'd rather make us come back."

"Your family is strange," he said. "Why wouldn't she take her? Not even for your sake?"

"There is so much bad blood between them," Alina said. She wondered what would happen to her mother if they had an accident on their way out of the country, if their car were to coil around one of those black silhouettes on the edge of the road. "I'll tell you about it, I promise," she continued. "Once we've crossed the border."

"What makes you think that Theresa will dig her out of the hole, then?" Liviu asked, turning toward her. His eyes had something fierce and cutting in them, as they reflected the light in the dashboard.

"Look at the road," she said. "Aunt Theresa will get her. If my mother dies, it would be on her."

"Would it?"

Alina preferred not to think about it. She had little choice—Border Security would have checked any bottled goods they found in her purse or in the car. It would have been impossible to spirit her mother across the border.

A plonk on the window interrupts Alina as she recites "Our Father who art in Heaven . . ." for the fifth time. Then comes another one, and another one, and Alina can now distinguish them for what they are. Not plonks, but the splash of raindrops on scratched glass.

Rain. Rain. Alina sinks from her chair onto her

knees and begins sobbing. Tears flow for the first time in the day that they've been detained at the border.

"God, no, please, not rain. Not rain."

She brings her moist forehead to the cold, dirty floor, leaving behind crushed hopes, regrets, and other bodily secretions.

Alina had been against marking the spot where her mother was concealed—she said it would attract unnecessary attention. Therefore, only a small mound of refined earth would show the spot. But not if it rained.

Rattled

I recite all the prayers that I can remember, beg the saints and Virgin Mary for mercy. I don't want my mother to die. I don't want to be the one who killed her. I make the sign of the cross, fall to my knees, hands clasped. My lips burn with the fervent whispers. *Please, God, help us cross the border, please stop the rain, please let me tell Aunt Theresa where she can find my mother, please don't let her die. Our Father, who art in Heaven, Hallowed be Thy name—*

The door opens with a violent creak, and a bald man with an oily moustache marches in. He grabs me by the elbow, forces me up on my feet. His fingers are claws in my flesh.

"What are you doing? Were you praying?"

I remember Peter's story, how he denied knowing Jesus when he was apprehended. God will forgive me, too.

"No! No! I wasn't praying! I was just tired."

The man grinds his teeth, then pushes me into the metal table. It screeches as I collide with it. There's a sharp pain in my hip.

"Body search," he says.

He turns me around, pushes me harder into the table with his knee. Its corner pierces my stomach. I wail. He catches the nape of my neck, squeezes hard. "Shut up!"

His hands move up and down my body, tear my shirt open. The callused tips of his fingers are on my waist, on my breasts, on my legs. He rips my nylon pantyhose.

"You're tired, huh? I'll show you tired!"

I can't breathe. I can't breathe. This is not happening. Not again. Hands tugging, grasping, pricking, smearing. His hands moving on my thighs, upward. I want to scream from the top of my lungs, until my vocal cords snap, but there's no point: If I scream, nobody will hear. I bite my tongue until I draw blood, and then even harder. I bite the tongue of this body that doesn't belong to me anymore.

Then, the fingers withdraw, without forewarning.

"Sit down," he says.

I wrap my cardigan around me. My skin is still prickling where he touched it.

"Comrade Mungiu, where are you and your husband headed?"

My tongue feels swollen and bruised. "To Aalen, in the Federal Republic of Germany," I say.

"Why would you seek West Germany? Are you attempting to betray your people and your country?"

I shake my head. I'm trembling. "We're not. My

husband is writing this research paper on Roman fortifications." I'm trembling. "It just happens that there are a few very well preserved—"

"Are you cold or are you afraid? Are you lying to my face?"

"I'm cold. I'm cold," I say, wrapping the cardigan around me tighter. During the body search, he tugged at my shirt, opening a few buttons. Cold air rushes on my exposed skin.

The man gets up and opens the obscured window. A freezing draft streams inside. I can see outside is pitch black. It was noon when we arrived at the border. My body convulses because of the cold. The man pulls his chair close to me. His moustache is in my face, almost touches my cheek as he speaks.

"Aren't there enough ruins in our beloved motherland, too? Am I mistaken, or weren't the Romans here, too? What would you want in the West?"

I lower my gaze, stare at my skirt. A thread has come loose, and I have an irresistible impulse to rip it. I wrap my hands around myself tighter. My foot jolts with the shivering.

"Perhaps you're meeting your brother-in-law there?"

"No! No!" I screech.

It goes on like this for hours. The same questions. Where are we going? Why? Where will we be lodged? How much currency do we have with us? Have we hidden objects of value we could swap for currency in the car? I can rest assured that it has been taken apart.

I keep fidgeting, shivering, glancing out the window. I think about my mother, imagining how scared and cold and lonely she might be. I whimper a "Please, let me go" after each and every one of my answers. We're going to Aalen. We're on vacation. We'll be sleeping at campsites. We have the prescribed amount of currency with us, and nothing more. We didn't hide anything in the car.

He doesn't know, he can't know that my most prized possessions are three coins: fifty Yugoslavsian *dinara* that jiggle in the pocket of my skirt. The money destined to be swallowed by the first pay phone we find after crossing the border.

Late into the night, the man finally gives up.

"Fine," he says. "Fine, I believe you."

I find it hard to be relieved. I say, "Thank you," though my words are barely audible because of the clattering of my teeth.

The man jumps up and darts out of the room. Tears begin streaming down my cheeks. It's over. I lay my head on the table, wondering if they'd mind if I doze a bit, until they finish the paperwork. Half-hidden, I finally close the buttons of my shirt. I didn't dare as long as the man was here, questioning me. I didn't dare irritate or provoke him.

I jingle the coins in my pocket. They're warm to the touch, smooth and irregular. They soothe me. I close my eyes. We have to hurry if we want to save my mother, hurry into the car, and into Yugoslavia. Hurry to the first roadside motel, or restaurant that is open, or hurry into the first village, or the first post office, and I'll call my aunt. I reach again into the pocket, seeking the familiar feeling of the fifty *dinara*, and they rattle, rattle, rattle their song, and I hope it's not a requiem.

Weeds of Truth

The door creaks. A tall, blond man with short-cropped hair comes in. He holds a passport in his hands and a few sheets of paper. I leap up to meet him.

"Thank you," I say, reaching for my passport.

He snatches it back. "What are you doing?"

The ground is spinning. I fall back onto my chair, unable to keep my balance.

He throws the papers on the table, leafs through my documents. "You have a visa for the Federal Republic of Germany," he says, pointing at it. "It's almost expired."

I try to focus, but I fail.

"Why the hurry to leave now?"

My mind rushes through the weeds of truth. I can't tear them out of my head and hand them to the man. I can't tell him that we had applied for different visas, that we had made different escape plans, but the fact that I was more or less raped changed everything. I can't remember what I was supposed to tell him. The relief wiped my head clean of the practiced answers. I should have made a list, recited it like a poem.

The man pounds his fist on the table. I recoil. The reverberations are transmitted to the foot of the table and into my body. I tremble again.

"Hey!" he says. "Answer me!"

"I . . . We . . . It's hard to obtain a visa, you know that," I say. My teeth clatter so hard that I can barely speak.

"So?" he says. His eyes, watery gray, stare me down, immovable. This is the kind of man who could drive a glowing-red pair of tongs through my entrails and not even blink.

"It's hard, it's hard," I say. "We wanted to go. To go. My husband's paper."

"Why didn't you leave in April, when your visa first came?"

I grip the corner of the table to steady myself. I'm so tired, and so hungry. The contours of the man become fuzzy, then clear again. I stare at the cement floor. I'd like nothing more than to lie down on it. Lie down. Just for a moment.

And the Earth Shudders

And I tell the Customs man, "We didn't leave straight away because of my mother. She disappeared earlier this year." I break into tears again when I think about her, and I bang my head against the table, and the man places a hand on my head, and his fingers brush my nape, and he says, "I didn't mean to upset you."

Because he's the nicest interrogator we've had so far, and he's nothing like the one before him, the one who did the afternoon shift, the tall one with his bitten nails and hanging belly, who threw a bucket of cold water on me when I rested my head on my chest after he left the room for a moment, saying, "I thought that you were thirsty," but I was so tired, so tired, I haven't slept in two days, not since they've been keeping us here, at the border.

And even if this nice man asks the same questions, he always waits until I stop whimpering to continue, and now he asks, "Well, but what if she returns while you're away and she can't find you?" I sob so hard that the air catches in my lungs and I can't breathe, because my mother may never return, because only I know where she is, because it's been too long, too long, and I jingle the *dinara* in my pocket, the ones meant to save her, and I wonder if there's anything in the perfume bottle in the ground worth saving, did she burrow her way through the lid, did her eyes begin to glow in the dark, does she see the wooden box where we buried her father, all those years ago?

I want to tell this kind Customs man that they've killed her with the questioning, that *I* killed her, and then it strikes me, that it never had to be this way.

"Yes. You're right," I say. "I need to go back."

I jump up, and the man startles, and I already have a list of things to do in my head: 1. go back to the first town, 2. find the first pay phone, 3. call Aunt Theresa and tell her where my mother is, perhaps she can still be saved, but I wobble, I must have leapt up too quickly, the room turns black, and I dig my hands into the table. I'm so tired, and I haven't eaten in two days, and the man asks, "What are you doing?"

By then I've steadied myself and I tell him, "You're right, I'll go back. Liviu will go alone to the FRG, and finish his paper. You're right, he doesn't need me, he can write it by himself. I must go back, go back to my mother, back to the first town, and never mind, I don't care if you let him go or not, but I have to go back."

The man grips my arm and frowns, and I can see he thinks that I'm mad, but who wouldn't be in my place? The fear, the hunger, the exhaustion, and then, what I have done, oh, why didn't I go back the first day, it would have been so easy. I wouldn't have killed my mother, I hope I didn't, and if I didn't, two days buried in the ground, she'll hate me forever.

The man leans in, whispers in my ear, "Do you know what will happen to you if your husband never returns? If he defects?"

And I throw my head back and giggle, and then hear myself laughing like a witch on the records with fairy tales I sometimes played for my pupils in school. "There's nothing left they can take from me."

The man steps back, and I hold the table tight so I won't fall, and he pushes my passport toward me. "Wait here," he says, and he leaves, and I don't move, and he's gone for a long time, but when he returns, I'm still here, gripping the table, and he motions me to follow him, and I put one foot in front of the other, fighting to keep my balance, like a baby who's trying to walk, but I'm so happy I could kiss him. I'll 1. go back, go back to the first town, 2. find the first pay phone, 3. call Aunt Theresa, and so I'll save my mother, I should have done this long ago, when they first started questioning us, and then I'm in the hallway for the first time in two days, and then Liviu is coming toward me, escorted by the man with the oily moustache who questioned me yesterday, and the Customs men, they bring us out, and take us to our car. And there we stand, both, watching them, and the nice man says, "Go, you're free to go."

"Where to?" says Liviu. He has blue circles

around his eyes, and I don't know if they're bruises or if he's tired.

And the nice man says, "You're free to go to the Federal Republic of Germany." He points toward Yugoslavia, and Liviu turns and jumps in the car, and I take my seat in the car though I don't believe them, this must be a trap, and the nice man leans toward me and says, "If I were you, I'd never come back. Don't come back." But I'm already gone, and Liviu revs the engine before starting it, and we're off, and there are no shouts, no shots, no second thoughts, just a white Dacia rushing into the night, swallowing the road beneath it, swallowing the road to freedom.

Epicenter

Alina spends the second day of Christmas, 1989, alone, in front of the television. Liviu has taken a job today. Someone's desperate to move into their new home by the New Year and wants the place painted. That's what Liviu does, nowadays—he paints walls in houses. His hands are raw with the lime. Weeping cracks that never heal cross the back of his hands. Sometimes, after dinner, Liviu looks at them, and wonders. He says his hands are foreign to him, that looking at them is like playing in a movie where he doesn't know the lines. And yet, of the two, Liviu is the one who grumbles least. It must be the two afternoons per week he spends presiding over his club of amateur archaeologists.

Of the two, Alina is the loneliest. It's afternoon, and she has nowhere else to be. It's dark as a pit in their two-bedroom flat. Alina browses the TV channels, stops to watch the news. Panama's dictator seeks asylum at the Vatican embassy. And there's a revolution taking place in Romania. Alina's heart pauses for a moment. Images unwind: muddy corpses, lying on white linen sheets in a field, lit candles at their heads, surrounded by weeping relatives. Ceauşescu speaks from his balcony in Bucharest—the crowd jeers. Ceauşescu escapes in a helicopter, the crowd takes over the building of the Central Committee of the Communist Party.

The commentator says that Romania is now a free country. As images of the apprehension, trial, and execution of the dictator and his wife unravel, Alina jumps to the telephone. There's nothing preventing her from calling her aunt, from speaking to her mother. They've corresponded through rare letters sent through four different third parties, to make their source untraceable. She hasn't called in thirteen years, careful not to cause trouble for Aunt Theresa— if they notice that she's receiving calls from the West, the Secret Services would tap her line. Alina hasn't talked to her family since the day after they crossed the border. In Austria, Alina telephoned for one last time, and Aunt Theresa calmed her: she'd found her mother; she's shaken, but otherwise fine; she's housed in the cage that once belonged to Alina's grandfather, as a measure of precaution, just to avoid any conflict with the cat.

Alina dials her aunt's telephone number—she's been repeating it to herself at least five times per day since they defected, to make sure she'll never forget it.

The dictator is lying on the ground, his face is as yellow as a wax candle, his eyes are open and staring into nothingness. Images of street fights in Bucharest begin to roll. Tanks parked in an alley shadowed by lime trees. Men in shirts and dark trousers—on the other side of the street a soldier, shooting. Alina wonders, how much courage do you need to charge into gunfire? The announcer talks about thousands of people killed. There are images from a hospital, the floor full of stretchers with wounded men and women, some of them naked, attached to all sorts of pipes. Some aren't even stirring. Alina clutches the telephone receiver, her knuckles turning white. These are the people who never ran. These are the people who fought.

Then, it's over. The announcer speaks about a panda in a zoo birthing twins, but Alina doesn't hear him. She wonders, why should she call at all? What is there to say to her mother? Her escape, the source of reciprocal accusations, apple of discord. And what does it matter whose fault it was, when people died, are dying, will die for freedom?

Alina smolders in her armchair. If it weren't for her mother ratting on them, maybe the authorities would have left her alone, even after Mihai defected. If her mother hadn't been so selfish, Alina would never have left. She makes a list of all the things she could have done during the revolution:

1. Been shot.
2. At least wounded.
3. Maybe dead.
4. Been a hero, in any case.

5. Done no less than clamber through a window of the building of the Central Committee, like a bug crawling out from the eye of a giant rotting predator, and she would have fluttered one of those flags all the revolutionaries were holding, the flags from which the emblem of the Socialist Republic had been cut, the ones with the hollowed middle, torn, not unlike Alina herself.

The Flight

I stop staring at my boarding pass (which says the same as it did two minutes ago: May 25th, 1995, From: Munich, To: Tenerife Sur, Boarding Time 11:15, Gate P30, Seat 22C) and then do as my husband does:

1. Store the rucksack in the compartment above the seats.
2. Fasten my seatbelt.
3. Play with the foldable tray.
4. Store my handbag under the seat in front of me (I stole this idea from the lady across the aisle).

Damn, now I don't remember if I ticked "check my lipstick" off the list I made at the gate. Looks good. Maybe I did, then. The announcement says *Check that your seats are in an upright position*, and Liviu has already done it while I was looking in the mirror. I don't know how to, and I'm not going to degrade myself by asking. I'm not giving him the opportunity to boast that he has already flown (once).

I'd rather seem recalcitrant and have the flight attendant admonish me. I deserve this because I messed up the other list.

Lately, I need lists a lot. They keep me from forgetting. I asked my doctor if you can get dementia from old people, but he said you can't. I'm still skeptical about that. Maybe I should have told him everything, but I was too ashamed. I'll make a list for next time.

Things to tell Dr. Braun:

1. That I spoonfeed Mrs. Muller.
2. That I also change her diapers.
3. That Mrs. Muller is heavily demented.
4. That by the time she was sixty-five, she couldn't remember the names of her children, and now she is starting to forget how to swallow. Maybe this kind of dementia is contagious.
5. That the smell of poop from the tips of my fingers never seems to go away.

Strike the last one. Maybe it's not important. But what if you can get it through the poop, like hepatitis? Or worms? My mother always told me to wash my hands. But somehow, I can never get them clean enough these days.

Liviu leans across me. He says, *If you would bend a bit forward? We're taking off soon. I want to straighten your seatback.* I hate it when he gloats like that. I hate it. When his face is close to mine, I make a list of the things we could have done with the money instead of going on this stupid vacation to Tenerife:

1. Invested in Liviu's teeth.
2. Bought a used car.
3. Moved out of the hellhole we live in.
4. Traveled to Romania instead, so I could finally explain myself to my mother, slash talk to her for the first time in nineteen years.

He says, *I'm so happy we're doing this. It will be just like the summer when we met.*
I dreaded as much.
A list of things that have changed since the last time I saw the sea:

1. My belly is wobbly and my boobs are sagging and even I don't want to look at myself in the mirror.
2. I have no hopes or dreams, but maybe some ambitions. I just want to get this over with.
3. I feel like an orphan.
4. I don't have a home.

Things that haven't changed:

1. I want men to leave me alone.

I don't have time to think of anything else because it's happening. The plane is gliding really fast and now it gives a jolt and my stomach turns upside down and I think it wants to make its way upward, like the plane. Liviu's hand on top of mine feels like a giant slug threatening to swallow it. Next time we're looking at each other's nakedness, it will be so hard to run from ourselves. I wish we had never arranged this flight. But I have prepared some shields:

1. A stack of books for the pool.
2. Two pairs of very, very dark sunglasses, to make him believe that I am sleeping on the beach, while I am looking at the sky, wondering if God will ever forgive me for what I did to my mother.
3. A bottle of sleeping pills, to take very early in the afternoon.

Postcards to My Mother

Postcard 1—A Village in a Frog-Green Valley, a
Mountain Behind It. Pfronten, Allgäu, Germany

Pfronten, October 12th, 1998

Hello (or hallo) Mother,
I hope this postcard finds you well. As
well as anyone who lives in a bird's cage, and
in permanent conflict with the cat (as Aunt
Theresa tells me), can be. If you're asking,
I'm doing well, too. The doctors are helping
me finally deal with the harm I've done in my
life. Maybe the postcard confused you—I'm
not on a vacation, I'm in a recovery resort
(not unlike the ones you used to visit for the
rheumatism in your knee), except this one is
for the nerves. After my divorce from Liviu
(you'll be more than happy to hear this bit
of information), I suffered from what you
might call a little "nervous breakdown."
They call it "mild depression" nowadays.

My therapist, Dr. Rielke, says that it's on account of so many frustrations I've been amassing for more than thirty years (starting with never finishing college, and up to the job as "carer" I've done since I defected, which is nothing more than wiping old lady arses. No joy there—most of my "customers" patronize me for being a foreigner, instead of being grateful.)

Postcard 2—A Wooden Cabin on a Green Pasture on the Slope of a Mountain, Surrounded by Sheep. Pfronten, Allgäu, Germany

Pfronten, October 12th, 1998

But I'm getting away from the point. Yes, the frustrations, the doctor said, the tensions in my marriage to Liviu (apparently I took too long to realize that we weren't fitting together. But you know how it is. You never really think of divorce as a possibility if you grow up with the stupid Romanian mentality. I mean, look at Dad. Really, for his own sake, he should have scorched the earth behind him running from you, a long, long time ago. Maybe he'd still be alive if he had). Yes, the tensions, and there was also the extreme guilt I felt toward you (though, really, Mother, who would turn on their own children and rat on them to the Secret Services? Who? Who?).

According to Dr. Rielke, I was not only depressed, but I was also showing obsessive behavior (making lists all the time in my head and panicking if I didn't get all the boxes checked. But you know how I am—I like to have things organized).

But, again, this is not the point of the postcard. Dr. Rielke encouraged me to make peace with my past, and allow myself to admit that I was wrong, and that I did wrong by you.

Postcard 3—An Edelweiss

Pfronten, October 12th, 1998

So here it is.
I'm sorry.
Love,
Alina

Harbinger

Sie haben eine neue Nachricht erhalten am 22 Oktober um 14 Uhr 10.*

"Hi, Alina, Aunt Theresa speaking. Adam told me that you called and wanted to speak to your mother. We received your postcards, honey, they moved me to tears. But I'm sorry to tell you—I don't know how—"Sighs. Breathes hard into the receiver. "I'm so glad you wanted to talk to your mother, after all these years. She would have been so happy, I'm sure." Sighs. "What I mean to say is that—Oh, how can I say this? Honey, your postcards came too late. There has been an accident involving the cat."

Sie haben keine weiteren neue Nachrichten.**

---

* *You have one new message received on October 22nd, at ten past two.*
** *There are no other new messages.*

Pink Fudge Frosting

My hometown feels like a tune played in the wrong key. Roast beef frosted with pink fudge. After twenty years, it's the same and it's not.

The sidewalks are full of potholes where dirty rainwater gathers. I can't see the bottom and still I know I am out of my depth—it's impossible for me to walk around here in my heels. I don't know how the others do it, these flocks of teenagers in slicker jackets and dizzying stilettos. On the streets, dark cars, Jaguars, Audis, BMWs sink their wheels in holes in the asphalt with great pomp.

The pharmacies, the department stores, the supermarkets have all changed. There was a pleasant pattern in that gray cement with tiny, white pebbles on all the floors. The communists used it everywhere—in hospitals, in stores, in factories. Now, there is too much light in all the shops, and it's infinitely reflected by shiny tiles in vivid colors. I wonder how their eyes don't hurt.

Even the apartment buildings are painted red and green and yellow, searing my retinas.

I flinch and cower in front of this cacophony of colors and light. If something's not colorful, then it's at least covered in plastic. Like the vegetable market. It's now a hall covered with a transparent plastic roof, but at least the metal stands are the same as thirty years ago. The women behind the counters have suffered the same process of plastification. The middle-aged women in straight knee-length skirts, with head-kerchiefs in floral patterns, have turned to wearing pink and orange tracksuits.

I'm buying some eggplants for Aunt Theresa, when I recognize the woman standing in line behind me. It's Mariana, one of my former fellow teachers. She pretends to be glad to see me while she eyes my manicure, my haircut, my posh slim-fitted dress. Her whole being appears to have had an unfortunate encounter with bleach.

She tells me how the news that I fled the country came as a shock. How she never expected it. How I was the opposite of daring. How she never expected that I would be so successful. *A house-cleaning agency? My, my!* She tells me she's happy for me. That maybe I always had it in myself—I did surprise everyone with that affair about the contraband magazine, didn't I? *People change, don't they?*

Do they? I ask. *You were ratting on me. That never would've changed, would it?* It's a shot in the dark, but her mouth shuts with an audible click and she scurries off, like a cockroach hurrying under the sink when you turn the lights on. I remain standing, feet well anchored in the ground, throwing a tall shadow over all the shrill colors around me.

A Wooden Box

Perched on the edge of her armchair, Aunt Theresa looks like an ancient bird of prey. An old hawk. Her back is bent, and her legs are curved—osteoporosis is unforgiving. The tips of her toes barely brush the polished floors. But what troubles me most is her face, the wrinkles like the deep furrows in the shell of the earth, like the ones I saw the day she drove me to the country. What also disturbs me is how lean she has become: her round, Botticellian thighs dwindled, the whole of her dried and shrunk like a raisin. I wonder what is draining her. I wonder if it's the old Romanian fatalism, which makes people barely past sixty arrange their own funerals; it's also a sort of modesty, not wishing to burden the ones who live on. I wonder if it's all because of her will to occupy a smaller wooden box when the time comes.

Aunt Theresa and I, we have sunk low. We used to soar in the high circles of kindred spirits. Now, our conversation has the plastic sheen of the fakes everybody in this country wears.

Our meeting starts well, then she says, "You should have called more often. I missed you."

I reply, "I should have."

This is the only moment of honesty between me and my aunt, before we veer into half-spoken truths, untold reproaches. I tell her about the cleaning company I started when I left the rehab clinic. About its success, and the empowerment it gives me. But I don't tell her that now, aged over fifty, it is the first time I have any kind of control over my own life.

My quiet brooding lays a blanket of silence between us, until Aunt Theresa says, "Never mind. Let me give you back your grandmother's earrings."

"Keep them," I say. "I can't remember one single instance when I've missed them. And besides, when I die, they have nobody to go to."

Aunt Theresa says, "I'll give them to my granddaughter."

"I think they'll look gorgeous on her," I reply, though I don't know her grandchildren, and I don't want to.

"*You* are beautiful," she says. "You're so much more mature."

"I recommend a divorce anytime instead of Botox or other expensive beauty treatments." I chuckle. "I feel twenty years younger."

In a way, this is true: living alone, using a dating service, this is not what I'd imagined I'd be doing at age fifty-five. But these are not things I could tell my aunt, not now, after having grown in an entirely different direction, a little Romanian tree malformed by the forces of the West. Soon, I won't even need my roots. There is one more offering to my past that I have to make, one more candle to light on a certain grave.

"Where did you bury my mother?" I ask.

Aunt Theresa sighs. She rubs her fingers together—they sound like sandpaper. She scrambles from her armchair, begins fumbling with her glass display. That's when I notice that all the cups are turned upside down, just like that time when she inadvertently called upon the *strigoi*, that troubled, bloodthirsty spirit. She extracts a wooden box, its lid encrusted with images of oak leaves, twisting together in the form of a spindle. She rests her wrinkled hand on it.

"Alina. I have a confession to make. I lied."

Aunt Theresa opens the box.

Acknowledgments

I'd like to begin by thanking the people without whom starting this book wouldn't have been possible: my husband, Silviu, and my mother, Claudia. Silviu, thank you for all your infinite support of my writing, and for believing that I had an ounce of talent. Mom, thank you for all the help with the research, and for always cheering for each and every one of my stories. Also, many thanks to my brother Cosmin, for reading and applauding every story I've ever written. As a writer, family support makes such a huge difference, whenever you battle with mountains of rejection slips, or if you just need someone to watch the baby while you have to take care of some quick edits (thank you, Mom; thank you, Dionisa).

A thank-you from all my heart to the entire Fairlight Books team: Louise, Urška, Gabrielė, Lindsey, Mo, Rebecca, and Emma for your catching enthusiasm and the love you treated my manuscript with. As an author, it's a joy to work with a team as dedicated, professional, and passionate as you are. Thank you, thank you, thank you.

ACKNOWLEDGMENTS

A basketful of thank-yous and hearts to the members of my writing group, Flash Force 5, for your unending supply of hearty support, sound writing advice, and patience. I learned so, so much from you wonderful, talented ladies: Christina Dalcher, Kayla Pongrac, and Stephanie Hutton. Stephanie, in particular, thank you so much for believing in this book, and being my "literary" shoulder I can cry on.

Also, thank you so much, Gillian Walker, for all the priceless feedback you gave me. Your opinion is always much cherished, and I love our little talks about the writing life.

A heartfelt thank-you to the editors who believed in individual pieces from my novella-in-flash, for selecting and publishing them in their literary journals.

The flashes first appeared in print as follows:

"Glazed Apples"—*Ambit,* January 2018

"The Skirt"—the 2017 National Flash Fiction Day Anthology

"Like Music"—*Flash Frontier,* February 2017; reprinted in the Paper Swans anthology *Flash, I Love You!*

"Prima Noctis"—*Litro Online*, #flashfridays, September 15th, 2017

"Ripping"—*Chicago Literati*, December 2nd, 2016

"The Low People in Our Family"—*The Airgonaut*, May 2017

About the Author

Sophie van Llewyn was born in southeastern Romania and now lives in Germany. She has published and won awards for her flash fiction and short stories across the United Kingdom, Europe, and the United States. *Bottled Goods* is Sophie's debut long fiction work. It has been long-listed for the Women's Prize for Fiction 2019, the Republic of Consciousness Prize 2019, and the People's Book Prize 2018.